Mr. Beethoven

PAUL GRIFFITHS

D0093865

 New York Review Books New York

This is a New York Review Book
published by The New York Review of Books
435 Hudson Street, New York, NY 10014
www.nyrb.com

First published in the United Kingdom in 2020 by Henningham
Family Press.

Extracts from *The Letters of Beethoven*, edited and translated by
Emily Anderson (1986) appear here courtesy of W. W. Norton &
Co., Inc.

LIBRARY OF CONGRESS CATALOGING-IN-PUBLICATION DATA
Names: Griffiths, Paul, 1947 November 24– author.
Title: Mr. Beethoven / by Paul Griffiths.
Other titles: Mister Beethoven
Description: New York : New York Review Books, [2021]
Identifiers: LCCN 2020058343 (print) | LCCN 2020058344 (ebook) |
  ISBN 9781681375809 (paperback) | ISBN 9781681375816 (ebook)
Subjects: LCSH: Beethoven, Ludwig van, 1770–1827—Fiction. | Handel
  and Haydn Society (Boston, Mass.)—Fiction. | Music—United States—
  19th century—Fiction. | Music—Classical influences—Fiction.
Classification: LCC PR6057.R515 M7 2021 (print) | LCC PR6057.R515
  (ebook) | DDC 823/.92—dc23
LC record available at https://lccn.loc.gov/2020058343
LC ebook record available at https://lccn.loc.gov/2020058344

ISBN 978-1-68137-580-9
Available as an electronic book; 978-1-68137-581-6

Printed in the United States of America on acid-free paper

10 9 8 7 6 5 4 3 2 1

for Anne

1 – The Cabin

"Mr. Beethoven?"

The person so addressed, lying in the narrow bed built into the far side of the small cabin, moved only with the gentle roll of the ship. Eyes and mouth were closed. There was no sound.

The boy, without stepping forward any further from where he stood at the doorway, his trailing hand still on the brass knob he had lately swiveled open, tried a louder call.

"Mr. Beethoven?"

Still nothing. Somebody had informed the boy the previous day, but he had forgotten, that the recumbent body before him never would be made to stir this way, not if he were to yell at the top of his voice, not if he were to sing out lustily in his emerging tenor the master's "Ode to Joy," a tune of which, of course, this boy would have had no inkling.

What to do? He had been told to accompany the passenger down a deck to the dining saloon, where he would then have to don an apron quickly before serving the cabbage soup and boiled mutton, if these were on the menu for the evening. He could not return empty-handed. Nor could he just stand there; he was already at risk of taking longer over this mission than the steward would have been expecting.

Could he have misremembered the name? No. The spelling would probably have foxed him, but he could reproduce what he had been told pretty well. Then he thought how stupid it was to imagine that the man lay still asleep only because he had been hailed by the wrong name. Any sound at all should have had him blinking awake. Even the click of the latch.

The boy did a loud cough, having first raised his hand to his mouth for politeness. He took it down – who was watching? – and coughed again. There was still no response, and the boy, with no means to know why this passenger continued to lie so still, felt a cool flush just under his skin. He had witnessed burials at sea, conducted by captains who put on their vicarage voices, captains who stumbled over the sentences, captains who turned sullen for the rest of the voyage.

He stood there, nothing happening, while down below the other cabin passengers would be looking about them with feigned nonchalance, and the steward would be standing smiling, a napkin over his horizontal left forearm, as if everything were proceeding quite normally, while inwardly the fellow would be calculating how the scale of remonstration would be rising with the this boy's increasing dilatoriness, hard second on hard second.

The boy let go the doorknob and took two steps further into the cabin, enough to be standing over the passenger. Behind him the door had closed, so that the cabin was notably dimmer, its only light seeping in through a small porthole. Even so, from this nearer position he could clearly see regular movements in the man's nostrils and hear a periodic disgruntlement coming through the slightly parted lips.

He leaned down close to the ear nearer him, taking care to keep his lips away from the alien flesh, and this time, so as not to alarm, whispered.

"Mr. Beethoven."

Still expecting a response, he was more than ever disconcerted, and may not have noticed, as he stood up, how puzzlement and anxiety about what was happening right there, in the cabin, were dismissing fear of reprisal below.

He reached out a hand. Could he bring himself? Yes, he could. Touching the man's arm, but through the bedclothes, and so protected from direct contact, he gave a firm, short push, and again repeated the name.

"Mr. Beethoven."

Yes, the eyes opened and the face came alive. The head turned a little, so that these newly opened eyes might look directly at the face of the one who had summoned them from whatever dream. The mouth opened, as if to speak, but then closed again without doing so, no doubt because the passenger realized that if he said anything the boy would be bound to answer, probably with a question – you could see from his look – and then what? The eyes closed again.

"Mr. Beethoven, you're wanted below for supper."

But the boy did not get far into that sentence before he remembered at last that this passenger did not respond to speech. Could he bring himself again to touch the passenger? He could – though it would have been too much to expect him not to use his voice at the same time, as if somehow to make the rousing more civil.

"Mr. Beethoven, please!"

It was as before: the eyes opened and the head turned. A stare, from a stranger, can be a flooding of humanity through whatever dams of difference, enough to make the boy feel he knows this man, better than he knows the captain, better than he knows his grandfather, that suddenly he has in his mind full possession of this person.

As he held the boy with those eyes, the man fumbled his hands out from under the bedclothes to grasp the nearby right hand of this new young friend. The boy felt the clutch and almost immediately a tug that would have unsteadied him had the grip not been relaxed right away.

He understood. Bringing his left hand into action, clasping as well as he could with his slender fingers the two rough hands still holding on to his right, he pulled the man up into a sitting position. Then, when he was sure stability had been achieved, he let go. The man nodded thanks, breathing heavily as he sat there, keeping himself upright with his two flattened palms pressed down on the bed. Then he swung, with no warning, his legs out of bed, and with an alacrity that took the boy by surprise, stood up in his nightshirt, a little shorter than the boy and evidently waiting for something. Yes, the boy would have to help him dress.

2 – The Dining Saloon

It may have been lit by a chandelier and lined with oak paneling that threw back a sheen, but these accouterments boasted vainly against the modesty of the dining saloon. Under the starched napkin that was now placed over his left hand, the steward raised and lowered his index finger in a gesture the boy recognized as conveying relieved acknowledgment that the passenger had successfully been brought down, querying displeasure that the bringing had taken so long, and monitory promise that the matter was by no means concluded. The boy smiled, and some of the other passengers, whose attention had been drawn from their soup plates by the belated arrival of their last traveling companion and his young escort, smiled back, before the sounds of silver dipping against china, and of more or less discreet slurps, resumed. This early in the voyage, the passengers were all a little wary of exposing themselves to conversation.

There would have been no real reason for the steward to move around the table to the one empty chair and pull it out, were there not the immediate need to make it clear to the boy that responsibility for the distinguished passenger had now passed from one to the other of them, and that the passing did not require any kind of communication. It was taken, what had not been given.

In this kind of society, the steward is very unlikely to have had any notion of the nature of his passenger's distinction. Even less chance that the boy would; he would have noted a tilt of the head or a raised eyebrow on the part of the steward sending him on his errand, and that would have been enough. It was distinction, the awareness of which may have made the boy all the more awkward in pulling and twisting the gentleman's attire into place, with little help from the sleep-softened body, which by now would have been seated at the table and begun venturing on the plate of soup placed immediately before it, venturing with a spoon and a slurp both almost certainly noisier than the others'.

Some of those others would, no doubt, have been more closely acquainted with their companion's accomplishments. Perhaps all of them were. They were, after all, cabin passengers, paying notably more than those stowed side by side below decks.

At some point there would have to have come, then, over the arhythmic percussion and subvocalizations of eating, another sound.

"Mr. Beethoven," the voice began, raised, as its owner turned from taking possession of the table to focusing on the late arrival, and then, recognizing that the latter made no response, and possibly remembering something, salvaged the intervention by changing it from an approach to an imparting of information, to be expressed at a lower level, with eyes now scanning the others:

"Mr. Beethoven is, I understand, traveling to Boston to attend the first performance of a new work of his."

This situation or explanation of the gentleman's presence, sitting there eating his soup while the others had stopped to listen to the speaker and were deliberately not looking at the person under discussion, could have been recalled from the pages of a musical magazine but was confided as if it had been private information. Taken as such, it would have seemed more to close the topic than open it, leaving everyone but the speaker to return to the rapidly cooling soup. After a moment, with spoon still lifted and eyes striving to keep back the appearance of disappointment, the speaker would have had to do the same.

It would be possible to work out which vessel this might have been, in whose dining saloon these people were delving into their cabbage soup with greater or lesser pleasure. Suppose the year was 1833, as could well have been the case; that would give the distinguished passenger enough time to have moved on from what had absorbed him almost exclusively through the mid-1820s: the string quartet.

Not so long ago, the task of finding what could have been this particular ship – one sailing for Boston in 1833 from continental Europe, and from a port that would have been accessible at the time from Vienna without quite some difficulty – would have presented, well, quite some difficulty: a trip to the headquarters of the National Archives, in Washington, D. C., or, after 1994, to that department's new facility at College Park, Maryland, where are housed, among other documents, passenger lists for vessels arriving at U. S. ports between the 1820s and the 1980s, these lists being printed forms, the earlier ones completed in neat, swift copperplate, presumably by immigration officials, detailing each passenger's name, age, sex, occupation, "country to which they severally belong," and "country of which they intend to become inhabitants" (given as "United States," or "U. States," or "U. S.," or sometimes "America," but, during the period in question, only rarely "U. S. A.").

Now the whole thing can be done at home. And it

can be done at no cost, thanks to the Familysearch
website supported by the Church of Jesus Christ of
Latter-day Saints – not, of course, for the purposes
of narrative fiction, but rather to enable adherents
of that faith to identify their ancestors, who, unable
in life to hear the word of Joseph Smith, may
nevertheless be saved if their descendants will stand
baptism on their behalf.

Skimming through the lists of the thousands
who disembarked at Boston in 1833, looking for
any names not obviously British or Irish, you
might seize on "Abraham Hultz," and so be led
to the brig *Florida*, which sailed from Amsterdam
with just seven passengers (leaving room, then, for
your imaginary eighth), curiously, all of them men
(family groups were more the norm) and relatively
young (which was not so unusual). Abraham, at
twenty, was the baby, and he – who had now given
up on the soup – tops the list, presumably because
he was first in line presenting himself to the
authorities, for there is never any evident reason for
how entries were ordered. Below him are Antoni
and Francis Kizer, thirty and twenty-five respectively, both of them coopers and, surely, brothers,
as might be confirmed by how they lift their spoons
in synchrony. Next are a shoemaker, a farmer, and
a baker – all useful trades where they were going
– the first of them the same age as Francis Kizer, the
other two twenty-eight. Last on the list was another

twenty-five-year-old, J. J. Whatson, mariner, with the observation: "put on board and passage paid by U. S. Consul." You might wonder if he, nervously darting his eyes around the table, was being sent home on account of some misdemeanor perpetrated in the Dutch capital – but why, then, as a cabin passenger, all expenses paid?

Apart from this Whatson, given as belonging to the U. S., the passengers are all said to hail from Holland – though this seems unlikely, given their names. Hultz, possibly Jewish, could have come from anywhere, though possibly not from the Netherlands, since there are no Hultzes listed in the online Netherlands phone book. Nor are any Kizers to be found there (the Massachusetts phone directory, by contrast, includes many more than could plausibly have been descended from this pair), but plenty of Keizers. Perhaps Harman Wibling, the farmer, also suffered mistranscription, for this is another surname unknown to the Dutch resource. Or perhaps he was the sole living representative of his line, emigrating to leave a trickle of progeny in Danbury, Connecticut, and Fort Lauderdale, Florida. (Unused to having a meal provided for him, he had already emptied his bowl by this point.) With Joan Floren, the aptly named baker, we at last have a potentially Dutch name, but not so with the shoemaker, Peter Wortley, who must have been British by birth.

Yet there they all were, on board the brig *Florida* (which, by the way, was to be painted in watercolor only three years later at Palermo, Sicily, the resulting picture to be sold, in Boston, by the auction house of Skinner, Inc., in 2006 for $8,225), bound for a new life from which, they must have thought, they would never wish to return – unlike their companion passenger, old enough to be their father.

Did each of the six, and the U. S. Consul, too, make separate arrangements with the captain? That they were all single men, and much of an age, might argue rather that they arrived as a group. If so, what brought them together, the possibly Jewish painter (Hultz), the two coopers, the very likely English shoemaker, the farmer, and the baker, all of them now awaiting with various shades of expectation the main course? They were skilled artisans, and would therefore have had some time for their own pursuits. Could they have been keen amateur musicians, the Hultz-Kizer-Wibling string quartet, joined by an English clarinetist and a bassoon-playing farmer? And the U. S. Consul, with some sympathy for his miscreant (who, his peppermint cordial spiked by laughing comrades, had been arrested for lashing out at a passing stranger), had placed him in this vessel, where, never separated from his French horn, he would be among friends. They could even get together to play their fellow passenger's Septet.

As for that fellow passenger, he could have reached

Amsterdam in stages, from Vienna to Salzburg, Salzburg to Nuremberg, Nuremberg to Frankfurt, Frankfurt to Cologne, Cologne to Amsterdam. The details of the journey need not delay the serving of the stewed mutton. The gentleman could have been there in a very few days; the others had perhaps arrived before him, awaiting the wind. And so the whole thing falls into place.

Some adjustment will be necessary, however, to what has already been surmised. A brig had only one deck, and so the cabin boy would not have been summoning the distinguished passenger from above but from along. And nobody would have been traveling steerage. The scene in the dining saloon (skip back from the mutton) could have proceeded as described, though you might have been imagining ladies present and there were none, and the one who spoke out would have had to be one of these young tradesmen. Even as such, though, he could have assumed a lordly tone beyond his years.

"Mr. Beethoven is, I understand, traveling to Boston to attend the first performance of a new work of his."

Let's say this was Peter Wortley. He was, of course, right.

3 – The Port of Boston

Entering the sound – sound!

"Entering the sound soon," said Peter Wortley –

No. This would have had to be the sailor aboard, whom they were by now all calling "J. J." (all the younger men, at least), the only one who could have been there before.

"Entering the sound soon," said J. J. "Then big city." He had been speaking right through the voyage in abrupt phrases, and the others did not know if this might have been his usual manner or something he did for their benefit, in the expectation they would understand him more easily. "Laid out before you," he went on. "A panorama. A real panorama. Just wait."

They waited. All forward. The seven young men. All straining their eyes ahead. And their distinguished companion. A little apart. Pacing.

Let's say it was springtime. The passenger lists do not record dates of landing, but let's say it was springtime. Early May. The wind on the water was enough for them to have their greatcoats buttoned, but the sun was up in a clear sky, and two or three gulls were calling into the bright air.

That wind, of course, was what was giving the ship its power, conveying them steadily west, between two of the outlying islands of the sound, for here we may travel faster than the wind and in these few lines have our eight passengers marveling at the vista laid out before them. A panorama. A real panorama.

But now we're moving too fast, because first they had to make their way among the vessels crowding the sound, some of them new arrivals, like them, some setting out, some crossing from one part of the harbor to another, some anchored, some following a shoal of fish, some spinning for pleasure:

Tjotters. Hoys. East-indiamen. Yachts. Gigs. Outriggers. Tepukeis. Trabaccolós. Hulks. Razees. Orkney-yoles. Ungalawas. Gundalows. Howkers.

A printed view from Corey's Hill, Brookline, offers what is perhaps a similar prospect, of variously sized boats moving in various directions or not at all, including a three-master, its sails lashed up, pointed southward right in the middle, being also in the middle distance, the sight of it just opened up by the passing of a smack steering in the opposite direction, while a pair of dinghies lie nearer in, close by the Brookline shore, containing fishermen who are examining their catch or preparing for the next day, unknowingly traversed as they are by one of the vertical creases of foxing where the engraving must have been folded a long time, or at least this copy of it must, held by the Norman B. Leventhal Map Center of Boston Public Library.

Bigger than most of the boats in the sound, the *Florida* had the might and the right to keep to its course towards the long stretch of quays and docks where the city met the sea. Largely hidden at first behind the multitude of boats, some gliding, others stationary, the city revealed itself in flashing glimpses between sails, sudden slices of warehouses and boatyards along the waterfront, with a mass of dwelling houses broken by the occasional larger square or garden rising beyond, some church spires inching – or, rather, millimetring – into the sky, and, clamped on the summit of the hill, elevating law and legislature above religion, the domed state house of the Commonwealth of Massachusetts.

J. J. may have seen here the approach of home, slowly coming nearer, not himself as approaching home, but as home itself, the place familiar, slowly coming nearer, bringing with it the lanes and alleys that, at some level of his being, he had never left. There were no Whatsons in Boston at this time, but had he spelled out his name that way as a joke?

Watsons there were aplenty. Yet even if Boston had not been his place of birth, it may have represented to him his native territory, glowing above the allure of alterity he could have felt on sailing into Canton or Cape Town or – say he stayed with this ship a while – Palermo.

For the others, advancing on Boston for the first time, advancing on a New World city for the first time, very likely advancing on a great port from its seaward direction for the first time, this would have been the same view, replicated in seven consciousnesses.

One, though, older than the rest, might perhaps have simultaneously had different thoughts running through his head, seeking out on the quayside, as the brig came in to dock, some ancient sea dog seated on a bollard with a pipe in his mouth, some fellow who, sixty years earlier, then a scamp of a lad, could have been in this identical place with an older brother to help topple chests of poor-quality Indian tea into the waters. And perhaps this curious observer on the deck also imagined a time further back, though not by much more than two centuries, a time when on the site of this great city – vanish! – were the smoking firepits and the tents of the Massachusett. Wonkŭssis. Pohkintippŏhkod.

4 – The Welcome-Party

How could this have worked? On Corey's Hill there could have been a signal station, enabling the news to be flagged to the harbor master, as he had requested, that the brig *Florida* had been sighted. The harbor master, waiting for this information but not knowing when to expect it, could then have sent a boy to alert Mr. Lowell Mason, who would now be hard at work at his bank desk.

Here would be the moment to say something about this individual. Mason had arrived in Boston only seven years before, but was already prominent among the city's musicians, not least through his position as President, from the year following his arrival, of the Handel and Haydn Society, the organization that had, but before his time, issued the invitation to the distinguished composer. By now he had passed the Presidency to Samuel Richardson, on the grounds of having excessive responsibilities, but that would not stop him. Forty-one years old, his hair – to go by an engraving that must date from close to this period – already gray but vigorously swept back, as if he were permanently butting a strong wind, Mason was a force.

At least, he would have to be imagined so. Someone who was to leave in his wake sixteen hundred hymn tunes could hardly be puny. He had already compiled his first book of these, adapted from the works of the European classical masters and published by the Society of which he was soon to become President.

Or all of this could be left for the moment, held in reserve to be discovered later, not presented right out as bald fact but dribbled into dialogue between two other characters. "I fear our Mr. Mason, though he has been in this city fully seven years, has yet to – ." That kind of thing.

But to continue: Like many of his time, a time when the notion of "classical masters" was as yet quite new, and needed defending, he held firm to what was sufficiently venerable to be venerated; and, of course, the name of the Handel and Haydn Society – founded by an earlier generation of Boston musicians, in 1815, when Haydn as well as Handel was securely in his grave – testified to this same steadfastness. Quite what he thought of the master he would soon meet he was not required to disclose – certainly not on this particular day, when he was writing in a ledger as the signal flags were hoisted on Corey's Hill.

Mason was, of course, by no means less prepared than the harbor master for the signal to come and, with it, the need to act. When told that some ragamuffin with salt in his hair had come into the premises asking for him, he went straight to the director's office. He had, some days before, forewarned this director of the guest he was expecting, and asked if he might leave at a moment's notice when the summons arrived. Permission had been freely granted – the director may well have had his own expectation, of an invitation to dine with the great man – but Mason considered it wise now to tell his superior that the moment had indeed come, and to confirm that he would not be missed for two hours. Care here was an absolute necessity, for though music was his great love, it could hardly make him a living. The director, his own hopes perhaps vividly in mind, insisted Mason take the whole day off, to settle the distinguished guest in his new quarters and make sure he had all he needed. Yes, he must go. Now. For Mason, though, there was no excessive hurry, as it could not take the boat less than an hour to come in to port. He had time to proclaim his thanks before striding outside to hail a chaise to take him home to Myrtle Street, on the "flat of the hill," as it was called, a few blocks north of the Common.

There, having quickly acquainted his wife Abigail with the wonderful news and told his coachman to make ready, he changed to his own vehicle and went off to collect two colleagues from the Society, since the greeting of the distinguished visitor, the first noted composer to venture to the Americas, could hardly be achieved with sufficient gravity and display by one man alone. This was a scene that history would want to replay; the pattern must be established with appropriate ceremony.

Mason therefore followed his long-laid plan and had his coachman drive not east to the harbor but north and over the Charles River to Washington Street, where the first of his confederates of the morning, Jonas Chickering, had a piano factory. There would be the opportunity here for atmospheric description. The journey took them through high-class residential and busy industrial quarters of the city, past the rattling of other carriages, the chinking of reins and bridles, hammering from five-story outfits producing furniture and tiles and brass bells and cogwheels, the smells of horses and smoke and steaming metal, the silent presence of a flower seller seated in purple woolens at a corner.

However, Mason, and then Chickering with him, noticed none of these things, which constituted the Bostonian's regular background noise. Besides, they had other things to do, and not do. They drove back across the river and south to one of the main thoroughfares leading down to the harbor, State Street, to collect Richardson, warranting his inclusion not only as the Society's current President but also as having been responsible, ten years before, for extending the commission to the one they were on their way to see come ashore.

Richardson was in every sense a large man, and his imposing figure, as well as his voice, had several times suited him for the role of Goliath in what was the Society's favorite oratorio of the moment, Sigismond von Neukomm's long-forgotten *David*. Chickering was more the typical character-tenor, quick and agile and small, while Mason could not have been anything but the conductor of this ensemble. All pinned on the name badges that Abigail Mason had made for the occasion, so that they looked like people attending a modern conference. They held back their excitement, perhaps, and the petty grievances they had, each of them with the other two.

But what can we know of all this? If Mason had taken command, it would have been because he was the most assertive and a natural organizer, though he might well have found some excuse, such as that his abode was well placed between the others'. They would not have wanted to quarrel with this, or else they would not have wanted to feel themselves in any way allies, even allies against Mason. There they sat, Mason with his back to the driver, facing the other two as if controlling their forward motion, as if their forward motion depended on him.

But this whole assembling of the welcome-party has to be understood as preparation and distraction in advance of the main action: the arrival. We are in a holding pattern, which could be continued with some account of what was happening aboard the *Florida* as her crew got her, themselves, and the passengers all set for the end of the voyage. For one thing, we should be clear about how the disembarkation of passengers was to take place. It is possible that the *Florida* would have anchored out in the harbor, and the passengers been brought to the quayside in a wherry. However, the arrival of such a person would need to be grander. A matter of him coming confidently down the gangplank from ship to shore. So let it be. So it was.

Mason and his two companions, having left the coach in Commercial Street, were ready. They had seen the fine ship, made finer by one among its human contents, gliding towards them, slowing as its sails were slackened, while being steered with perfect skill in the direction of Lewis Wharf. As they observed its approach, they made their own, stepping through the algal slime and the fish guts to the space for which the ship was evidently aiming, giving no mind to the men carrying on their backs baskets of cod or crabs, sailors calling from the rigging, moored sloops and schooners, a dog gulping down something, and that other canny canine seated on his bollard.

When they had reached the stretch of Lewis Wharf where the ship looked likely to put in, they stopped and again, for the last time, or for the last three or four times, practiced their greeting. They had decided, weeks before, that the occasion would demand a welcome beyond the usual, and had determined that each of them should offer the great man a brief salutation and then bow, the three of them in turn. After much discussion, the following program of events had been settled upon: first, Richardson would cry out "Herr van Beethoven!" and bow; next, Chickering, whose German was by far the weakest, was to add "Maestro!" and bow; then, Mason would bring the tripartite apostrophe to a conclusion with "Willkommen in Amerika!" and bow. That the estimable visitor would hear nothing was beside the point; they were to speak these words to the ages.

There is still a Lewis Wharf at Boston, but standing in what was then ocean, for the city has oozed out in the mean time, extending itself over wrecks and rotted wharves. The point where Richardson, Chickering, and Mason were standing is now well away from the water, somewhere in the region of Golden Goose Market. Rehearsing their performance at that spot did not cause any alarm or even draw attention, as they knew it would not. The lost and forlorn will slide toward the sea, and harbors are full of strange people, some of them liable to bind you with a sob story, ask for information you have no patience to give, or try to sell you a share in a ship they tell you is coming in from China. Best to ignore them and keep moving.

"Herr van Beethoven!" "Maestro!" "Willkommen in Amerika!" The three gentlemen were now, perhaps, going through their routine less from the need to practice than for the fun of it, and to relieve the tension of the moment as the brig came closer. There might have been the odd embarrassed laugh before they coughed and patted their coats smooth while the ship came alongside and was tied up. Then they all turned to scrutinizing those gathered on deck. Though they had seen no engraving of the great master in profile, he was easy to spot, his gray hair flying as a banner of seniority. The other passengers and crew held back as he came first down the gangplank, did not follow until he safely had both feet on the quayside. If anyone had offered to assist him, the kindness had been politely declined. He stepped down alone. And the three there to greet him stepped forward to line up before him.

"Herr van Beethoven!" said Richardson, and bowed. "Maestro!" said Chickering, and bowed. Neither of them could therefore see how Mason departed from the script. "Willkommen in Amerika!"

He let the words peal forth, and then, twitching his head to one side with a little snort, thrust forward his right hand. The distinguished disembarkee, unused to this form of civility, clasped him around the neck, kissed him firmly on the cheek, released him, and stood back smiling. Quickly recovering, Mason returned the smile, and waited for the great man to utter his first words in the New World. By now, Richardson and Chickering, too, were upright, and what they all heard was, of course, delivered in German, though the usual convention will generally be followed here, of translating anything spoken or written in another language.

Before speaking, however, the long-awaited master looked from one to another of them, then held Richardson with his gaze. He would be the one. The bigness of the man. The combination of formidable strength and naked vulnerability. This would be his protagonist.

Then his look lightened, and he spoke:

"Well, you can now see and know that I am here."

5 – The Room

"We hope you will be comfortable here."

Abigail Mason had not spoken these words, knew she should not speak at all, and was very content not to speak at all, but rather had conveyed them by a slow, low sweep of her right arm and something close to a smile, almost a smile, as she held the great man with her eyes before turning away to depart.

It is as if she disappears behind a curtain. She has supervised the preparation of the rooms the gentleman is to occupy, probably for the next five months. In recent weeks, she has been in here daily, to check that the carpet was smoothly laid back without creases, or to exchange one pair of ewer and basin for another that she thought finer, or more suited to a gentleman, or to refresh the pot-pourri, or to open or close a window. She needed to know she could not have done more. Now she would go, and not enter this space again until after their distinguished guest had gone. ("Our guest" is how she would speak of him; the first person plural was far more frequent in her thoughts than the singular.) Olwen would be in here, of course, to clean, to remake or change the bed, to empty the black-lacquer box of crumpled paper beneath the writing table, to open or close a window. But she herself would not. That would be improper.

So she disappears behind her curtain. We know very little of her, have no image. She was five years younger than Lowell, this Abigail Gregory, as she originally was. They were married fifteen years ago and more, and she will stay his wife until he departs this world almost forty years hence, after which she will remain his widow ("Widow" is the commonest occupation in the 1833 edition of the Boston Directory published by Charles Stimpson, Jr.) for another seventeen years, until her own demise at the age of ninety-two. By that time she will have seen her sons flourish, or not. A piano maker. A publisher. A composer. The black sheep.

There they are now: Daniel Gregory, named after his grandfather, aged thirteen; Lowell Junior, nine; Billy, four; and Henry, a year and a half. Be quiet now. And keep out of the gentleman's way. You are not to come in here. I have told you.

In a family such as this, there will, of course, be a nanny for the younger children. Almost certainly a cook, too. The maid Olwen and a manservant,

Bobby, must be surmised. All paid – Boston despises slavery – and some or all of them quartered on the top floor.

Overseeing them will be part of Abigail Mason's existence. What else? Is she, too, a musician? A singer, perhaps. Charitable work. Reading and writing letters – to an aunt, a sister. A lot of thinking, unspoken and unrecorded.

For lack of information, she dwindles into a stereotype. There must have been more. It has gone. She has disappeared, behind a curtain.

Ask life to speak of her and of a thousand generations of our ancestors.

It will not.

Left alone, the distinguished guest looked around him. This would be his abode for the coming months. It was all very satisfactory, more than satisfactory. A great effort had been made. This touched him. He could live here. He could work here.

What do we need of a room?

First, that it set a limit to space but not confine.

This room was well proportioned, with a high ceiling.

Second, that it be apart.

This room was its own little world.

Third, that it contain all the necessities, in due arrangement.

The writing table, solid but gracious, was

against the wall opposite the door through which one entered. It would be a waiting friend. On it at present were a lamp and an inkwell, with space for enough besides. In drawers the gentleman would find a sheaf of music manuscript paper, a supply of blank sheets on which to write notes or letters, some pens and a knife, bottles of ink, black and sepia, a piece of pale green blotting paper. Ready in place was a chair, with a padded leather seat.

To the left of the writing table stood one of Chickering's square pianos, one of his favorite daughters. They knew, of course they knew, of their distinguished guest's affliction. But their delicate inquiries, made through the banking network between Boston and Vienna, had indicated that the great master would still go to his instrument from time to time as he worked, to feel in the muscle of his hands, as well as in his inner ear, the contour of a theme, the spacing of a chord.

The window, filling much of the wall further to the left, and having a small table set with three chairs before it, gave on to the garden. Lace drapes soften the light.

Continuing anticlockwise around the room – if he could be imagined standing in the middle of it and slowly turning, now that he was alone – to the right of the door giving entrance was a generous sofa, sufficient for three people, perhaps four. Against the fourth wall, the one facing across to the window, was a smaller sofa and a chest of drawers, balancing one another on either side of the fireplace, of which he might be glad towards the end of his stay. A grand armchair stood close to him, inviting ease.

No pictures. Abigail Mason would have considered this, of course, as she considered everything. To put up one of their portraits – they had good engravings of Haydn, Mozart, and Bach – would have seemed presumptuous and might even have given offense. Who were they, so far away, to claim allegiances that were this gentleman's own? A landscape, then? But who knew what sort of scene their distinguished guest would wish to survey, day after day? A lake in the Adirondacks? A cow pasture beneath a heavy sky? Or what about a plan of the city? She had tried these and probably more, but everything had seemed to impose, to be a source of noise where she wanted quiet. The bold wallpaper was a little out of style, but it would have to do, broken by the doorways and wall lamps – doorways in the plural, for to the left of the piano, in the corner of the room, was another door, giving access to the small bedroom and, beyond that, the water closet.

Such was his domain.

Having taken it in, he touched the back of the armchair, but then turned his eyes to the writing table.

6 – The Breakfast Table

"Why can't we speak?"

"Papa has told you."

"Would you pass me the butter, please, my dear?"

"Papa just spoke."

"He was asking for something, Billy. He was asking for something."

"That's quite sufficient, Henry."

"I'm asking for something."

"Billy, will you please listen to your mother and keep silent?"

"Yes, Billy, shut up."

"Daniel Gregory, that is no way to speak to your brother."

"Sorry, Mama."

"And the requirement of silence applies to you as well."

"Yes, Mama."

"Could I have a piece of muffin?"

"And?"

"Please."

"Not until you've finished your potato, Lowell Junior."

"But I said 'please'!"

"And I said 'no'."

"Why can we not have silence around this table?"

"Please – excuse – the – children – sir."

"Recommend Virtue to your children; that alone, and not wealth, can ensure happiness."

"Quite so, sir. Could I trouble you for some more coffee, my dear?"

7 – The Writing Table

It must be surmised that the composition of his "Biblisches Oratorium" [1] was largely complete before the composer left Vienna, though there remains the possibility that, knowing he would be spending a month or more on board ship with very little else to occupy him, he may have set aside passages to be worked on during the voyage. The reported condition of certain sections of the manuscript, especially in the second part of the work, might have argued in that direction.

Beyond doubt, however, he left some details to be

---

[1] The *Morgenblatt für bildete Stände*, a daily newspaper published in Stuttgart and Tübingen, led its edition of November 5, 1823, with an article on the composer that concluded by looking forward to, among other works, "ein Biblisches oratorium ihm durch den amerikanischen Konsul in englischer Sprache aus den vereinigten Staaten überschickt" [a Biblical oratorio in the English language commissioned from him for the United States through the American consul].

settled in Boston, for this, at such a late date, was the first occasion that found him writing for resources far from the city of his permanent residence. He cannot have imagined, of course, that he would be able to hear his intended soloists and so compose specifically for their voices, as he may have done in former times, the first version of *Fidelio* being a case in point. Even so, he seems to have wanted to meet these people – to see them, to observe them in action, to gauge their ways of expressing themselves – before finishing off their arias, to the extent that one may still speak of arias with respect to what was evidently in every way an extraordinary score. The striking, and several times remarked upon, arrival of an obbligato viola in the central section of the orchestral introduction, announcing one of the work's most powerful and important lyrical themes, seems also to have been an afterthought, not present in the original draft, and it would appear likely that the adjustment – more than an adjustment – also dates from the months the composer spent in Boston preceding the first performance. Attempts have been made to identify the musician for whom this obbligato might have been written, but, unfortunately, surviving records give very few indications of the instrumentalists who took part in this notable première or who would have been available generally to play in the orchestra for Handel and Haydn Society presentations. Copies of the Boston

Directory for relevant years list, for example, a
French flute teacher (Dalmas) but no viola player.
Indeed, the term "viola" finds no hits on electronic
searches of these documents.

A much weightier question is that of the voice
type the composer was considering for his principal
role. With hindsight, of course, his choice of a low
bass might seem obvious and even inevitable, but
sketches predating the Boston months may show
the composer writing for a high baritone or possibly
low tenor, the unusual tessitura suggesting that
here he was recording his memories of some specific
singer he had heard, perhaps from as far back as his
teenage years in Bonn.

Magnificent as this role is, as finally achieved,
what may be judged an even more important matter
is implicated here, for, as the composer worked
on this part – and there are phrases in the revised
libretto of which he may have made up to seven
different settings – his style surely developed in a
radical and unexpected fashion. One might venture
to say that these various drafts would have conveyed
him gradually but nevertheless startlingly into his
so-called "fourth period."

The vexed matter of the dating of the score, and
of the sketches and drafts leading up to it, might
perhaps have been resolved, if only a little, by studies
of the various kinds of paper on which the composer
made his notations. However, this episode in his

life has been neglected in relevant studies,[2] perhaps because the surviving documents are so evidently incomplete. The composer must have brought at least a small stock of paper with him from Vienna, if, as we presume, his plan was to continue to work on the oratorio during the long sea journey. Even so, a large proportion of the finished score seems to have been written on bifolia acquired from the Boston firm of Grant & Daniell. It was probably also from this source that the composer acquired what was once known as the "Mason Sketchbook," on account of its descent through Daniel Gregory Mason to the actor John B. Mason, who sold it to Harvard University.

Now one of that institution's treasures, this octavo notebook, of sixty-four pages contained between covers of thin gray card, preserves sketches for parts of the oratorio as well as for other works the composer must have achieved or at least begun in Boston. Among these is the "Grand Suite," that being the amiably ironic title the composer gave to a set of six easy piano duets he wrote for the older Mason boys, Daniel Gregory and Lowell Junior. The finished autograph manuscript of this opus must also have been left with the Mason family, but

---

[2] The reader will search in vain for any mention of the Boston oratorio in, for example, the otherwise comprehensive investigations of the composer's working practice published by Lewis Lockwood.

if so, that document has been lost, and the work remained unknown, apart from the fragments notated in the Mason Sketchbook, until a copy was found in 2016 in the attic of a Boston townhouse. It seems likely that the Mason boys' duets were widely circulated among musical families in Boston, and it may be that other copies will surface, making it possible to check certain curious features in what is at present the unique complete source. Some scholars have ascribed these anomalies to misreadings on the part of the copyist, others to the composer's humorous imitation of the two young boys' hamfisted efforts to play his music, or to his identification, equally comic, of certain lacunae in their theoretical training. Since similarly bizarre harmonic junctures appear here and there in the altogether curious G flat minor piano trio that was one of the works the composer wrote soon after returning to Vienna, there is the possibility that he remembered the junior Masons' musical malapropisms, and even that, now assimilated, they had a crucial bearing on his later style.

There is no time now to consider the "Ocean Symphony" *(Sinfonia oceanica)*, whose origin may similarly be traced to the Harvard Sketchbook. Discussion will also have to be left for later of the set of songs in English that was yet another fruit of these productive months.

8 – Early Concerns

"Do we know what he's up to?"

"The oratorio."

"I know, but have you seen any of it?"

"Not as yet."

"Have you asked?"

"These are early days. He spends all his time in there, with his door closed. Sometimes, as you pass, you can hear the vigorous scratching of his pen. Or a groan. Or a thump on the table. Or – not so often – some majestic sway of harmony on your piano, Chickering. B flat major most of the time, I fancy, this last day or two. Before that I'm not sure."

"But you haven't actually asked to see the score?"

"It's difficult. You know how it is communicating with him. As far as I'm concerned, he must know how eager we are to make the acquaintance of this colossal masterpiece. He must know we want to start some trial rehearsals. He will tell us when he is ready."

"Until then we wait?"

"Until then we wait."

"And we introduce him to those from whom he may choose his solo artists –"

"A preliminary afternoon has already been planned, for Thursday of next week."

"I thought it was supposed to be largely finished before he got here."

"I do hope there may be something for Mr. Colburn."

"Largely, yes. Waiting for some finishing touches. He wanted first to meet and to select – even if he could not hear – the singers for whom he would devise the solo roles."

"What you have described sounds like more than finishing touches. We may be in trouble here. This whole thing may end up never being finished. Or even properly started. If you say you haven't seen anything of the score, how do we know there is anything to see?"

"I am absolutely sure there is no need for anxiety…"

9 – Possibilities

Say the composer is sitting in his armchair, now angled away from his writing table so that he can see, seated on the room's pair of sofas, five or six young women the Society has enlisted as candidates for the solo female parts in the coming performance. Our best guide as to their identities has to be what is known of the Society's concerts during this period, perhaps drawing again on the Boston Directory for confirmation and supporting details, but all this may be left for another time, when the singers are called upon to sing. Here they are just being inspected. The audition, if such it may be deemed to be, is silent. The composer will very likely turn his head from time to time, to look at one group or the other, or to focus alarmingly on an individual. And perhaps, with a nod he will gesture that individual to stand, and will raise his arm to call for a turn of the body, even a walk around the room, under his gaze, the other candidates no doubt striving not to watch, still less scrutinize. All this without a word. He will not speak. He does not want to encourage them to let slip their guard for a moment and, to their lifelong embarrassment, speak to him, as if they could speak to him, use the voices he cannot hear.

Alternatively we could go to another moment from around the same time, when the composer – what could be more natural? – is taken to see one of the two German-born members of the Society: Gottlieb Graupner, who was among the Society's founders, and the organist Charles Zeuner, who last year wrote an oratorio himself, *The Feast of the Tabernacles*, though this has yet to be performed.

"I wish you could have met Mr. Heinrich," – this must be Chickering – "such an interesting man, wayward perhaps, but, yes, interesting. It is such a pity he has lately returned to Europe."

Graupner would be the only person the composer could be meeting in Boston and finding to have not only the same mother tongue but also much the same cultural formation. He is a little older than his visitor, perhaps stiffening and rising weakly from his deep green armchair as the composer is shown into his parlor. A warm embrace may be imagined. Of the two men's conversation, however, only one side will remain: Graupner's, written down on a sheet of paper in the form of questions and remarks to which the composer would have responded vocally. It was an old practice of his, but one to which he seems to have resorted, during these months in the United States, only on this single occasion, perhaps for the very reason of the common language.

How could such a record have come down to us through two centuries? Perhaps it was Abigail Mason who kept it, to the end of her ninety-two years, and bequeathed it to her grandson, another Daniel Gregory Mason, composer of a string quartet that appeared on an LP recording. So close these people are, yet beyond reach. Perhaps to Abigail Mason, long after these events, the sheet seemed to speak of them aptly by its silence, by its evidence of the great master's presence and simultaneously of his absence, of what was said to him but not of what he said:

Es tut mir sehr gut, Sie wiederzusehen.
[It does me much good to see you again.]

*

War's nicht in Hannover, daß wir uns vor fast einem halben Jahrhundert getroffen haben?
[Was it not in Hanover that we met, almost half a century ago?]

*

Ja, wirklich. So musste es in London gewesen sein.
[Really. Then it must have been in London.]

*

Ja, wirklich. Ich dachte, Sie haben unseren lieben
Haydn auf seiner Reise begleitet.
[Really. I thought you accompanied our dear
Haydn on his journey.]

*

Wo war es dann?
[Then where was it?]

*

Es macht nichts. Wollen Sie etwas Kaffee,
Schokolade?
[It doesn't matter. Will you have some coffee,
chocolate?]

*

Erzählen Sie mir bitte etwas über dieses neue
Oratorium, auf das wir uns alle so sehr freuen.
[Please tell me something about this new oratorio
we are all so much looking forward to.]

*

Sechs? Nicht mehr als das?
[Six? No more than that?]

*

Sehr klug. Erinnern Sie mich an das Thema.
[Very wise. Remind me of the subject.]

*

Und die Stimme Gottes?
[And the voice of God?]

*

Nur Sie, mein alter Freund.
[Only you, my old friend.]

The page here comes to an end. There must have been more, of course. Perhaps it was just this page that reached Abigail's hands, having been brought back as a memento by her husband. Or perhaps she had more in her possession and distributed them to her several grandchildren, some of whom could have been less careful with them than Daniel Gregory, or given them away or sold them to persons now untraceable.

Alternatively again, we may be taking the wrong tack entirely in going on with scenes that create themselves around the obstacle of the composer's deafness. We need a way through, and ahead.

10 – The Real Truth

How about this? Boston provides the composer with a means of communication not available to him in Vienna. Here she is now, standing in his room. Abigail Mason is introducing her, one hand placed against the small of the girl's back to offer support, in a gesture the girl appreciates but does not really need, the other passing the composer an envelope. He takes it, slowly tears it open. In it he finds a short note. Both he has been expecting: the note and the girl. The note, of course, is lost, along with so many other ephemera, souvenirs that would have given us the thrill of a physical connection with these events. The composer reads – no doubt the writing is Lowell Mason's, in his most careful German – and at one point raises his eyes to look at the young person before him. Her eyes are on him. She is not wary, not fearful. He nods, and returns to the note.

Her name, then, is Thankful. *Dankbar.* Through her hands he will hear – hear music, no, but hear what is being said to him, this he will. Her hands will open a door on to the silent noise of conversation. She will teach him her sign language.

Impossible? No.

Everyone Here Spoke Sign Language:
Hereditary Deafness on Martha's Vineyard
(*H.U.P., 1985*) - Nora Ellen Groce

Based on her doctoral dissertation, Groce's exemplary study reveals that there was a sign language in use on Martha's Vineyard by the early eighteenth century, if not before, necessitated by a rare prevalence of hereditary deafness, which peaked around the time of the great composer's visit to the region, when it affected around one person in a hundred and fifty, rising to one in twenty-five in the village of Chilmark, the phenomenon, general and local, being easily ascribed to the in-breeding that will occur within an island population and particularly among those in an isolated settlement. Some of the aged people with whom Groce spoke during the course of her research, their memories going back into the nineteenth century, if by no means as far as the time of the great composer, recalled how deafness was so common as to be unremarkable. A person might be remembered for other attributes and anecdotes before the interview subject would recall that, yes, he or she was deaf. Almost everyone in Chilmark would have had at least one family member who was deaf, and so almost everyone would have known some sign language, which could be useful even for communication between persons with no hearing impairment – for example, for silent chit-chat in church. Groce records a society in this respect Edenic, where deafness was no handicap, whether socially or in terms of education and employment.

What Groce cannot record, of course, is the nature of the Martha's Vineyard sign language in its pristine form. From 1817, deaf children from the island were educated at the American Asylum for the Deaf, which opened that year in Hartford, Connecticut, and which provided a development site for what became known as "American Sign Language," based principally on the French system brought to the school by Laurent Clerc. Children arriving with their own sign language, such as those from Martha's Vineyard, who accounted for a sizable proportion of the roll, may well have contributed to the new language, but we cannot know to what extent.

The importance of Martha's Vineyard, then, is not that it possessed a distinct sign language but that many of its hearing citizens would have been adept signers, and therefore a translator might plausibly be found who could, having taught sign language to the important visitor, convey to him by signs what other people wanted to say to him. Such a translator would not have needed to know the important visitor's native language; what the one signs "in English" the other understands "in German," and vice versa. The lack of detailed information about the Martha's Vineyard sign language is of no account, for prolonged descriptions of hand signaling ("holding the right forearm raised perpendicularly with thumb and forefinger touching as if holding a pen, the middle finger concealed behind the thumb and the two other fingers placed flat against the palm, while with the little finger of the left hand...") would only slow us down.

Yes, we have all we require to summon an interpreter from the island – a girl in her mid-teens seeming most likely, out of school and as yet without commitments, happy to take temporary employment relaying messages to and from the important guest. And it will be easier if she can hear and speak, and so be his ears and mouthpiece for conversations anyone might wish to have with him. Those in day-to-day contact with him, such as Lowell Mason, might almost forget she is there, the process of transmission and retransmission becoming so natural. Us too.

We can bypass how this young girl is found on Martha's Vineyard and brought to the city, perhaps through contacts made by some member of the Society in the shipping business, to be met at Boston harbor one May morning of her sixteenth year by Olwen and so silently or chatteringly walked up, with a basket containing some good clothes and whatever treasures, the two of them passing some buildings that, venerable then, can still be seen, including the Old State House, from the time of King William III, and King's Chapel, on their way to Myrtle Street.

The noteworthy guest has, of course, been prepared for the encounter. It will have been explained to him in writing that a girl will be arriving and joining the household as his amanuensis – not in any musical sense, for he needs no help there, but as his assistant in communicating with other people, for, dear sir, as you may have been informed, there is a region of this commonwealth where a system of hand signs has been developed so that persons who have lost the faculty of hearing, or who never had it, can be spoken to thereby, without any need for writing, such as I am doing now. So let it be. So it was.

Having by now reached the Mason residence and been admitted, Thankful is separated from Olwen, with whom she had begun to form an attachment, and taken by Abigail Mason up to meet their distinguished guest. Or perhaps he is out on some visit or errand – at Chickering's piano factory, for instance, or at the paper store of Peter C. Jones & Co. on State Street – and will be returning for lunch, so that Thankful will have to wait some while in the kitchen, where she is given a cup of broth, before she can be accompanied upstairs for the scene with which this chapter began.

In the interim Abigail Mason has withdrawn. The composer beckons Thankful to come nearer, and she does so. They are of a height. Having by now learned the drill, and feeling it should be applied universally, he offers his right hand, which she takes and lightly strokes with her other hand, her fingertips passing over veins and knuckles. She stops, instead points at the hand she is still holding, lets it go, and executes a sign. He does not catch this, and is about to speak when she performs another sign he easily interprets as admonishing silence. She takes his hand again, points at it, makes the sign as before. He tries for a second to contain himself before a guttural groan escapes his rapidly shaking head and spittle flies. She repeats the sign slowly, does so again, and then once more at speed. He looks at his own hands, jerks them up to clasp his face, and groans again, into them. She will not have this. Wordlessly she reaches for those hands, gently guides them down again, looks at him to command attention, and tugs them into making the shape they must. He repeats the sign on his own. And again, faster. Big smile. Big smile from them both.

How many days, how many weeks, would it have taken for Thankful to demonstrate the rudiments of Martha's Vineyard sign language and teach the great master a usable vocabulary? There will be moments of awkwardness and suspicion, resolved when Thankful does something to make her pupil laugh. And then those guffaws will be heard again, through the days or weeks, shaking the house. Abigail Mason, carrying a tray from parlor to kitchen, looks up. There may also be long intervals of silent concentration, the visitor staring at Thankful's hands and agile fingers as she shows the differences between, let us say, "bread" and "five," or some other pair of words easily confused.

Of course, this Thankful will need to have some knowledge of musical terms. Right. She started piano lessons when she was four and is by now a very capable musician. She may even have gained from her teacher an acquaintance with music theory and have entertained herself inventing signs for "Picardy third," "six-eight time," "échappée," and so on, with no-one on whom to practice these gestures but herself. As to her keyboard skills, she has long outgrown her infatuation with the "Moonlight" Sonata (some of that thrilling mental gape she will feel again in a few years' time when she discovers Chopin) and now prefers Op. 109. She is sensitive to the irony, and surely pained by it, that, for the very reason she is here, in this room with the great composer, with one of Mr. Chickering's finest instruments over there, she will never be able to play that sonata for its creator and have him hear her. Yet perhaps there will come a moment when the composer, entering his room quietly for once, catches her at the keyboard and recognizes from the movements of her fingers – fingers he has been observing with keen attention for another purpose – what she is playing. See him smile. See him step back silently out of the room again. Or see him wait until she has reached the end of the piece and place his hand so gently on her right shoulder.

How many days, how many weeks, would it have taken for Thankful to demonstrate the rudiments of Martha's Vineyard sign language and teach the great master a usable vocabulary? Well, it is over; it is done. But they go on practising. The great composer is right now intently studying the shapes and patterns Thankful's hands are describing, almost as if they were talking (at times, he thinks he can hear her voice, which is not like the voices of mouths but more like the low register of a clarinet – a point of

some relevance to the obbligato for that instrument
in a movement that might easily become, at some
future date, the adagio of a concerto, the great
interlude of self-communion that follows the
central character's one solo in the second part of the
oratorio), and talking not only to him, those hands,
but to each other.

11 – Portrait of Thankful

It has to be a girl. This was the unconsidered assumption from the start, and must be right. It has to be a girl, for a girl they would think more patient, more reliable, and surely more likely to fit the august visitor's paradigm of helpmeet. You would like her to have red hair, another feature that might easily be the product of in-breeding. Hers is not the acid orange of a carrot-top but auburn, the rich, darkened red-gold that a spectacular fall season may place in a leaf. Her intelligence – a requisite, of course – is visible at this moment not so much in her mouth, which she is holding closed, not tightly but firmly, against the risk of giving something away, perhaps a feeling, perhaps a hope, as in her eyes, over whose glisten, even when motionless, she has no similar control. Coming from Martha's Vineyard, she is probably going to have to be the daughter of a family whose wherewithal comes from farming or fishing, her father off by himself for long periods in some corner of field or ocean, her mother nearer the house, tending animals (we may see pigs, a golden cow) or gutting herrings for smoking, neither of them having so much time for the child, or the children if there are more than one – and if there are, then maybe Thankful is a junior mother to the younger, which might account for her enclosure within herself, her guarding of herself, though this aspect of her will also, whether there are younger children to oversee, older children to wonder at, or no siblings at all, come from her bookishness. The family is not impoverished, but there is little to spare for anything beyond the regular household expenses. However, perhaps there is a free lending library in one of the isolated towns set up by a former pastor of means who had no offspring to whom to leave his books, and perhaps Thankful, on the weekly or twice-weekly expeditions by cart to buy and sell, could have won the right, by rare persistence, to go in and exchange one book for another. Does she have any books of her own? You might want to think so, and think, too, that she has brought them with her in that basket, not so much for safekeeping, as she knows very well they would have been perfectly safe at home, of interest to no-one but her, and not because she thinks she will ever read from them here, for she knows she may very

well not, during these months (have they disclosed
any kind of a schedule? or is she traveling with no
end in sight while they hurtle toward a destination,
or rather feel that destination hurtling unsparingly
toward them?) in the city, where she has come to
enter a life so different that she cannot imagine
what will and what will not be possible for her, but
rather because she cannot let herself be parted from
them, would pine as for a pet. What might they
be, these books? A family Bible willed to her by a
maiden great aunt, with whom she found herself
in a sympathy neither of them could understand or
explain. *Pilgrim's Progress*, of course. An anthology
of poems. Something unexpected – a wheelwright's
manual – and we do not know how she acquired
it, perhaps because she does not know this herself.
Four books, then, let her have, and they will quite
likely be still at the bottom of her basket, unseen by
her or anyone else – known of, though, by her, by her
alone, a secret she must keep, for it is hers, as so little
is. It is almost as if they are warm, that they warm
her, lying there at the bottom of her basket, that
they warm her partly by their status as possessions
– or, rather, that they stay warm, like precious eggs,
kept warm by the clothes she has placed on top of
them, in her basket, within this tiny room they have
given her, no larger than a linen cupboard, and
perhaps serving as such until they had Olwen clear it
out and equip it with a small mattress, a stool, a jug

of water, a basin, a cup. And yet even these simple necessities are altogether more than we need, for we are straying from the purpose of this chapter, which was to sketch a portrait of Thankful. Thankful. Thankful. Hold her still. We seem to be seeing her against a dark background, a background so dark it is impossible to tell whether this is black or gray or brown, and whether it contains any objects – a piece of furniture? – or is all shadow. We might think we are looking not at her but at what is already a portrait of her, just of her against the dark, with her watchfulness, her life, and with her hair in seeming movement, against the dark, away from the dark, into the dark, out from the dark, but then who would have painted a portrait of a girl who is doubtless, when her duties here are done, going to return home to Martha's Vineyard and marry a farmer or fisherman like her father, and keep all this in the past, never talked of, but taken with her, on through her life, with her books and her music? No, this cannot be a painting. This must be the girl herself, in her stillness. And if this is enough, let her be.

12 – Return to the Scene

We may now go back to the illustrious guest's room in the Mason house at the time when five or six expectant sopranos – six, let it be – are still waiting to find out what it is that will be expected of them. No doubt drawn, or drawing themselves, from the city's affluent professional class – wives, sisters, or daughters of members of the Society (which is, of course, an all-male institution, as institutions tended to be) – they all of them take on the same posture, sitting upright, differentiated only by their clothes and their hats, for probably they would be wearing hats, out of respect.

How Thankful participates in this scene we may ignore. She is the great composer's ears, and her hand gestures no more need be described than would, were the transmission direct, the vibrations of the stereocilia. Let her be. Again, let her be. Let her listen, and form her own judgment.

But yes, let her listen. The great composer cannot, of course, hear these waiting, aspirant singers. But imagine this, that the extent of his deafness is not generally known. And imagine that he has, even in a few days, as it might be, come so much to trust Thankful's musical acuity that he will rely on her to adjudicate among the hopefuls. She will be in this respect, too, his ears. The singer will sing, and the girl will listen, and the unrivaled master will seem to be listening, and the girl will convey to him, as in the course of communicating whatever the singer is saying in response to a question, her findings. Unstable intonation. Shrill above D on the staff. Round, full tone and good feeling; maybe this one. And the great composer, who, observing closely all the while how the singer holds herself, how she walks, her facial expressions, will have been drawing his own conclusions as to the moral worth of each candidate, which is as important to him, of course, as the quality of her voice, will respond always with the same words: "I thank you."

The audition is over, the choice made. One of the singers is delighted, but, she would have to confess, not unduly surprised. Two are not really surprised, but nevertheless a little disappointed. One does not know whether she is surprised or not, being so much overwhelmed by relief, since she would never have put in for this had not her mother insisted. One is affronted. And one has only the barest sensations of pleasure or sorrow, surprise or unsurprise, for she is quite sure (and she is right) that Ignatius Plumer is on the point of proposing to her, and she thinks, yes, she is going to accept him.

13 – An Infinite Conversation

The Reverend Ballou, minister, huffing, puffing, up Belknap towards Myrtle Street, huffing and puffing because he is late, having been unable to break off the conversation to which he was summoned by Samuel Richardson, huffing and puffing because he is twenty pounds overweight or perhaps even thirty, huffing and puffing because he is anxious about this meeting face to face with the Orpheus of the age, huffing and puffing because he is lolloping uphill, huffing and puffing because the afternoon is sultry, huffing and puffing because he has no idea why he has been asked to take tea with the great man at two o'clock, which is already eight minutes ago, and the gradient is not slackening, and something Mr. Richardson said is slowly coming to bother him, and he really ought to cut out his housekeeper's nut cake, or at least take a smaller slice, or a good helping only every other day, comes Hosea Ballou.

There would be no need to relate how the Reverend Ballou, minister of Second Church, on School Street, arrives at the house to be admitted by Bobby and taken up to the waiting composer, who had no doubt informed Lowell Mason and thereby the household that this visitor was to be expected. We may, rather, go straight to the distinguished visitor's room. Once the Reverend Ballou has entered, the distinguished composer, alerted by Thankful, rises from his desk and, the custom by now well learned, shakes his librettist by the hand. It is not clear if this is their first meeting. If it is, then the great master is assuming a good deal of common ground, and even of connection, simply because he has for many months been working with this man's words before him and in his head. Of course, that raises the question of the esteemed composer's knowledge of English, a language he had never set before, his only preceding works with English texts being folksong arrangements, where, of course, the setting of the words was a given. The newspaper report of ten years before mentioned an "American consul" through whom the commission from Boston was imparted. But was there still such a consul in Vienna when the great composer turned from his eight third-period quartets, someone who could examine the growing draft and offer advice on matters of stress, rhythm, and vowel quality? The first permanent U. S. ambassador to the Habsburg court was appointed in 1838, too late for us. Perhaps the role of sounding board fell, then, to the British ambassador, Sir Richard Wellesley, who was in Vienna from 1823 to 1831, difficult as it may be to imagine a British aristocrat, the Duke of Wellington's younger brother, being able to read a late manuscript of the composer's and comment usefully on matters of musical setting. But you never know.

This matter has, however, left the great composer and Ballou shaking hands for far longer than necessary. Even if, presuming this was indeed their first meeting, a certain amount of gladsome exchange of greetings would be natural.

"The rooms look out on the garden," the composer said, turning a little to his right and raising his right arm toward the window.

Ballou, a scholar, having no trouble with the composer's mellifluous German, at once replied: "How very pleasant" – and of course Thankful was there to convey his remark efficiently to her gentleman, with a twist of one hand in another and a sweep of three fingers along the forearm, perhaps adding an ironic flourish all her own. Ballou was of an age with the composer, just four months younger. It may be less relevant that he was among the most formidable Unitarian divines of the period, and a proponent of universal salvation, his collected sermons, recently published at the time, stoutly defending that position.

"Yet garden air is just the very worst air for me," the composer said, having turned back and now facing Ballou directly. Flustered, the reverend sir shuffled with his coat and sat down on one of the sofas. As the great man remained on his feet, however, and had offered no invitation to sit, after a brief moment Ballou abruptly stood up again, to be motioned with an abstracted air to resume his seat. When he had done so, the composer, too, sat down, in his armchair. Ballou waited.

"Well, on the whole it is not at all bad," said the composer.

Ballou considered – hoped – that the composer would expatiate on this, and so maintained his silence.

And indeed the composer did go on: "Except the first act, which is rather insipid, it is written in such a masterly style that it does not by any means require a first-rate composer."

Ballou opened his mouth, and hesitated. How was he to take this? A negative remark – that word "insipid" (*fade*) stung, but perhaps, he tried to tell himself, it was just an unfortunate choice, on the part of a man whose forte was notes, not words (after all, he might have thought by now, that was why he, Hosea Ballou, was there) – and then what could have been construed a compliment, though it might be a double-edged one, all depending again on a single word that could, once more, have been hastily and ill chosen: "require" *(erfordert)*. Was the paramount master really telling Ballou that his libretto was so fine that any numbskull musician could make a great work of it, that the words would lend their luster to the music, no matter how mediocre the latter? Or was he implying, all this about "masterly style" ironic, that Ballou's text did not rise to the peaks that a first-rate composer would expect, to stimulate and support music of the greatest moment?

Well, Ballou could not sit there forever with his mouth open and the great composer staring at him in expectation of some response – and this girl, too – and so he closed it again before, having swallowed, opening it once more to speak, but was stayed now by the composer turning in his chair and leaning back to pick up three or four sheets of paper from the desk behind.

"Why did you do *so?*" said the composer, pointing at a particular line or pair of lines with his left forefinger as with that hand he passed the page to Ballou.

Ballou, who had read through his libretto several times during the morning in preparation for this meeting, recognized the episode but could not immediately think how to respond to the question. One has many reasons for writing as one does. The original Biblical text, of course, one keeps always in sight, also the need to interpret that text for an audience in Boston in 1833, to give it a certain Unitarian inflection, to follow a very simple verse form, to maintain a sufficiently elevated language, to write something one considers, from one's knowledge of the hymnal, will sing well. What precisely was the great composer questioning?

So long was Ballou taking to respond that the muses' champion spoke again: "I really can't get the hang of this."

That was not good, definitely not good, no question about it. Ballou looked again at the lines seemingly under dispute. There seemed nothing complicated or difficult about them, but he could not continue to sit there in silence with those two pairs of eyes – the composer's increasingly perplexed and demanding, the girl's turning to a hapless sympathy he might have felt even more discouraging, given her age and status – waiting for him.

"I think the point here," he began, and having begun found himself speeding up, his words cascading, almost beyond his control, "was for the character to express, to be expressing, or at least to seem to be expressing, some mixture or amalgam, if I might put it so, of feelings, as wonder and contempt, or hope and, as it might be, anxiety as to the outcome of that hope, or the possibility of that hope's having a positive outcome, however that might be judged, or even the desirability, or perhaps more exactly in this case —"

There a quick glance from Thankful asked him to stop, or at any rate slow down, since the language of signs could not keep pace with this verbal torrent.

"I'm sorry," he said. "To you. I mean, to you. I'm sorry."

"Say no more!" said the composer, and now they were both silent, until Ballou decided the injunction need not prevent him trying another tack.

"The number is in two verses," he ventured.

"The first is in D major, the second in E flat major," the composer divulged.

"Indeed," said Ballou, not quite sure what to make of this, but determined to proceed, somehow. He looked at the text and then back at the composer, who was shaking his right hand and blowing through slackened lips.

This done, the composer spoke again: "A good deal will have to be altered." And he added: "That is what is holding me up at the moment."

Ballou stared again at the sheet of paper in his hands, and, still looking down, began "The words here —"

The composer cut him off: "It is very beautifully written."

This was good.

"But it is all in vain."

Not so good.

What was the problem, though? It piqued him that this number was one he was proud of. Within its short space, in his view, he had allowed the central character to express his whole moral outlook.

"Could we, I wonder," he said, "go through the number line by line? You see, it was my hope that in this piece we could allow the central character to express his whole moral outlook."

"The devil take you," said the composer, "I refuse to hear anything about your whole moral outlook!"

Ballou fell silent once again. The composer – the great composer, the universally acknowledged master of the age, *his* composer – sat there, leaning forward, fury in his face. How had this come about?

It would be game of Ballou now to go on.

"I believe I can see," he began carefully, "how the first line –"

" 'What comfort can I give you?' " the composer quoted, before adding emphatically: "Fish-oil!"

Then his fury suddenly turned to furious good humor, and he was still laughing as he went on: "I am sorry," he said, "for both of us."

"But please give me some indication," said Ballou, "of what should be altered."

"I leave that to you to decide," the composer replied, and stood up, at which Ballou did the same.

The master took a step forward and seized Ballou's hands in his.

"Think of *me* when writing your poems. Do what you can."

Having said that, he turned and shook his fist at the window.

Ballou, aware that the interview was concluded, withdrew.

– Except that we might want to have him come back, because it could all so easily have gone a different way.

"The rooms look out on the garden," the composer said, turning a little to his right and raising his right arm toward the window.

The reverend sir looked that way, too, and sniffed, at which the composer, seeing a twitch out of the corner of his eye, turned back to face him directly.

"Yet garden air is just the very worst air for me," the composer said, motioning his ally to sit.

"Thank you," said Ballou. Then, when they were both sitting and looking at each other, the composer went on.

"Well," he said, "on the whole it is not at all bad."

Evidently, the composer was now opening the discussion, and Ballou waited for him to continue, as he did.

"Except the first act, which is rather insipid, it is written in such a masterly style that it does not by any means require a first-rate composer."

"Thank you," said Ballou warmly. Let us suppose

he had heard "*fade*" as "*Pfade*" (paths), and drew the conclusion he was being complimented for breaking new ground. Or perhaps he did not hear the questionable word, or unconsciously suppressed it, to smile on the phrase that followed.

"Thank you, indeed," he might well then have said. "I cannot tell you what a joy it is to me, my dear sir, to hear such words from you, for I have to tell you that when I was first approached in this matter, by Mr. Richardson, I hesitated. Indeed, I hesitated a good while."

"Why did you do so?" asked the composer.

"Because," Ballou replied, "you are who you are. You are – well, you are the author of pianoforte sonatas I have studied and admired from my youth. You are the master of the Septet that I and a group of my friends got together to play again only last week – I wish you had been there." Suddenly realizing his faux pas, he rushed on to his crowning apostrophe: "You are the genius of the symphonies to which the world resounds!"

The muses' champion raised his left palm toward Ballou, then turned his head away and sighed. "I really can't get the hang of this," he said. "Say no more."

Ballou paused. "Forgive me," he said. "May we then proceed, my very dear sir, to the libretto? I had a question about the two arias for the protagonist in the opening act."

"The first is in D major, the second in E flat major," the composer divulged.

"I see," said Ballou, not quite sure what to make of this. "I was rather expecting," he continued, "a minor key for the second aria. Possibly F sharp minor in that case, with the mediant relationship..."

The composer nodded. "A good deal will have to be altered," he said.

"The choice of keys," said Ballou, "is so important."

The composer nodded again as he spoke: "That is what is holding me up at the moment," and he reached back to pat the stack of loose sheets on the desk behind him, perhaps a hundred or more, saying as he did so: "It is very beautifully written." His hand came to rest. "But it is all in vain."

"Oh, my very dear sir," said Ballou, "do not say so! We may not always understand where our artistic genius is leading us, but we have to trust it, put our faith in it as the scintilla of the divine that is placed within us. Indeed, that is central to my whole moral outlook."

"The devil take you," said the composer, "I refuse to hear anything about your whole moral outlook."

Ballou was silent. How could he bring solace to this troubled soul?

After a full two minutes, he spoke again, very softly: "What comfort can I give you?"

The composer, whose head had been sunk, raised it again to look at his interlocutor. "What comfort can I give *you*?" he said.

"It is a comfort, my dear sir," said Ballou, still very quiet, "to be sitting here with you."

The composer's reply was almost inaudible: "Fish-oil."

Ballou could say nothing. The composer reached back again to put a hand on the pages of his manuscript. "I am sorry," he said, "for both of us."

"Would it help," Ballou began, with more energy. Could he say this? "Would it help if we were to begin all over again, my very dear sir, with a fresh libretto, perhaps on a different subject?"

"I leave that to you to decide," the composer replied, and stood up, at which Ballou did the same.

The master took a step forward and seized Ballou's hands in his.

"Think of me when writing your poems. Do what you can."

Ballou gently pulled his hands away and left.

– Except that we might want to have him come back, because it could all so easily have gone a different way.

"The rooms look out on the garden," the composer said, turning a little to his right and raising his right arm toward the window.

"And my friend Mason's famous delphiniums will now be at their peak," said Ballou.

The composer looked across at him uncomprehending.

14 – Continuing Concerns

"Then you still have no idea how much has been achieved since he came here?"

"No."

"He has volunteered no information?"

"No."

"And you have not asked?"

"No. Perhaps I should have done, at an earlier stage, but so much time has passed, so much silence that cannot now be broken."

"Let us recapitulate what it is that we *do* know. He has been interviewing singers?"

"Yes."

"And some have been definitely cast?"

"Yes."

"How many?"

"Two ladies, thus far. Miss Belcher and Mrs. Long. Their names are in my written report."

"Will they be all?"

"All the ladies? I believe so."

"But they have not seen their parts?"

"It would be a dreadful pity not to have something for Mr. Colburn."

"None of us has seen anything."

"He has also had meetings with Mr. Ballou?"

"Mr. Ballou has been once to my certain knowledge. He may, of course, have paid other visits when I was at the bank."

"But Mr. Ballou, too, has seen nothing of the score?"

"Mr. Ballou, gentlemen, is not the easiest person to inquire of."

"Indeed. But he has vouchsafed nothing?"

"No. We go on hearing these strange wide deserts of harmony and their occasional thunderstorms, and the dear man's grunting an octave or so below, so, yes, he is working – he is working all the time when he is not down at table with us or taking a walk on the Common."

"But you have seen nothing of this music?"

"Nothing."

"What about the girl?"

"My dear friend, I hardly think it would be proper for us to use her as our spy."

"I was not suggesting as much."

"In any event, she may have no facility in music."

"Oh no, she has. We hear her as well from up

there, at your piano. It is not difficult to discern her different touch. But she plays only sonatas and variations of his. Things we know. Sometimes a melody that might conceivably be part of the oratorio."

"You have not asked?"

"As I say, it would hardly be seemly."

"So all we know is the subject?"

"All we know is the subject."

15 – A Sale

... is he here of course he's here he must be here look over there is that not him no that's Dr. Shurtleff but he must be somewhere in the room you say he looks like President Jackson no no I said he's the same age as the President more or less but that must be him but a good deal shorter of stature and no now that he's turned somewhat stouter just coming through that the door may be him have you seen him before in the far left corner next to shorter you say the bronze

LOT 2. DEMOCRITUS AND HERACLITUS; Or the Laughing and Weeping Philosophers, the former smiling, and the latter railing at the follies of mankind. The figures are three fourths lengths, larger than life. An original, purchased from the collection of St. Severin.

from a letter from Washington Allston to Samuel Taylor Coleridge; Cambridge, Mass., July 24, 1833

I should tell you also about the sad sale of pictures from the estate of our much lamented President Jefferson, held last week at Chester Harding's gallery in the town – sad as so many sales are sad, dispersing to the whims of chance, opportunity, and wealth what a man has accrued around himself, like an animal its shell, to manifest in an outer harmony and beauty the shape of his very self. But it was sad also by virtue of how far the great man's taste, in matters of fine art, fell below his judgment in other domains of human affairs – and yet I do not know if this was entirely true of Mr. Jefferson, for a mind surely cannot be so sagacious in politics and lack the power to discern the sublime when it is presented in oils on canvas. I would prefer, therefore, to ascribe the poor quality of the works on view to the advice the late President received from those in whose connoisseurship he placed his trust, most especially Mr. John Trumbull – or "Col. Trumbull," as he was dignified in the sale catalog, on account of the few hours' service he rendered the Revolutionary Army. Of the colonel's own paintings I will say nothing. But his finger was evident not only in the fidgeting forms and dull colors of those pictures labeled as his in the exposition but also in the indomitable ordinariness of many others that he persuaded Mr. Jefferson to acquire in Paris. We were children, you and I, at this time, but it is not difficult to imagine how packed that city's salerooms must have been with magnificent objects as the Revolution advanced from premonition and rumor to actuality. Instead we find in Mr. Jefferson's collection, and I will give you only one example, a wretched and indistinct double portrait, on a scale that must only amplify the want of vivacity, intelligence, and, I will add, wit exhibited by two philosophical gentlemen of ancient Athens, the subject taken from Montaigne.

LOT 12. JOHN ADAMS. An original by Browne, taken in London, in 1785.

from a statement by Mr. Parkman
It is a fine picture, perhaps the truest likeness that exists of the nation's Second President, and after almost two centuries I remain very satisfied that I was able to buy it. The artist's name, of course, was "Brown," "Mather Brown," and the painting fixes a crucial connection and a crucial time in the history of our country – a connection between two of our early Presidents and a time when the gunsmoke of Revolution drifted in mid-Atlantic, having left our newly liberated States and preparing now to settle over France a while. The year was not 1785 but 1788, and John Adams was in London as our nation's first ambassador to the British court. Mather Brown had been there some years, one of many young artists

sent across the sea at that time and later to study with the Pennsylvania-born, London-favored Benjamin West. Also in the city was Thomas Jefferson, as a member of a delegation dispatched to Europe to negotiate loans and trade agreements. Jefferson had Brown paint a likeness of Adams, which he bought, and in friendly return, Adams commissioned Brown to make a portrait of Jefferson. The Adams portrait went on to descend through my family, though without my heirs remembering quite which of their forebears had purchased it. I might be the Reverend Francis Parkman, or George Parkman, physician, or Daniel Parkman, deputy sheriff. I suppose it is also possible I am Sally Parkman, listed in Stimpson's as "mantuamaker" – a manufacturer, that is, of ladies' formal robes in a very much antiquated style. And there are other Bostonian Parkmans of the time. Enough. I preserved a particle of history, and it has preserved a particle of me. Many more, multitudes more, were not even that fortunate.

LOT 27. DAPHNE, TRANSFORMED INTO A LAUREL. Apollo is seizing her round the waist, to bear her off, but her father, the river-god Pineus, who is present, transforms her in that instant, into a Laurel, the branches of which are seen shooting from her fingers. On the left are two female figures, struck with dismay, and also a Cupid flying off in consternation. The figures are whole lengths, that of Daphne of twelve inches; on canvas; an original; the subject from Ovid's Metamorphoses, Lib. I.

over that must be there him where in that far I can't
corner are you with the sure with the gray hat he has
which corner that right or left girl with him

LOT 28. JOHN BAPTIST. A bust of the natural size, the right
hand pointing to Heaven; the left, deeply shaded, is scarcely
seen pressing his breast, which is covered by his hair, flowing
thickly over it – seen almost in full face – on canvas. Copy from
Leonardo da Vinci.

note from Mrs. John W. Davis to her husband,
District Clerk
The Leonardo altogether too gloomy. Secured a
rather splendid landscape – river and mountains
– will fit over fireplace in D. room. Please give boy 2¢.
My sweet.

LOT 30. THE PASSAGE OF THE POTOMAC THROUGH
THE BLUE RIDGE. By Roberts.

from the diary of Israel Thorndike, Jr.
July 19, 1833. A little before ten o'clock I arrived at
Mr. Harding's Gallery in School Street to find a press
of people, many more of them gawpers than having
intention to buy, as it was to turn out. There is a lure
to the reliquia of the estimable deceased – these
were the late President Jefferson's paintings that
were being sold – whose better part is reverence and
whose worser a manner of vulgar curiosity touched
with ignoble satisfaction that the great one, too, has

been brought low. I feel these things in myself, and would rid myself of them. But we are all human, and have within ourselves the stars and the filth. The auctioneer was Mr. Cunningham, standing at his desk on a dais. Mr. Harding stood behind him, growing gloomier as the morning proceeded. I bought a puzzle. I bought a painting whose subject, as intended by the artist, has not come down to us. It is very evident that the artist did have some strong intention in the matter, for the persons are caught in attitudes of vigor, and there would seem to be something of life-or-death consequence going on. More than one such thing, it may be. Passions are high. But we do not know what they are, or what has provoked them, or how these people may be related one to another. Viewers are as if thrust into a theater, in the midst of the action, and find themselves deaf. One has to live with a painting. I will enjoy living with this one, down whatever years Providence will allot me, pondering my picture's ambiguity, which I might even feel to contain a kind of truth hidden to exactitude. The item is to be delivered on Friday. I will install it in my study. Before passing on to the events of the afternoon, I should copy out Mr. Harding's description of what I may now call "my" painting, so that I will know where to find these details, such as they are.

LOT 42. AN ACCUSATION. A group of nine figures of about one third the natural size. It is an original, on canvas, known to be by Solimeni, but the subject is not certainly known. It is believed, however, to be taken from Ecclesiastical History, and to be the story of a young woman accusing a young man, before a Bishop, who is sitting in judgment on him, and raises a person from the dead to be a witness.

he was here but he left

LOT 56. CHRISTOPHER COLUMBUS. Copied from an original in the Gallery of Medicis at Florence, for Thomas Jefferson.

from Chester Harding's ledger
in toto . . . .$ 452 & 38 ¢.
Disappointing.

16 – Going Away (1)

If the distinguished visitor was not at Harding's
Gallery on July 19, that was because he was spending
the summer with me, Josiah Quincy III. I belonged,
I may say, to the very highest levels of Boston society,
by virtue firstly of my birth, for I was the great-
great-great-grandson of an Edmund Quincy who
had arrived in the primitive town from England in
1633. Such things mattered, not only by reason of
the prestige accruing to us from the depth of our
implantation in this new land, but also because,
having come early, we had been able to acquire so
much of it. Let there be no mistake: the land was not
just grabbed from the unsuspecting natives; it was
paid for. Edmund Quincy's son, another Edmund,
purchased from the local population a tract of
territory south-east of Boston. We have the deeds,
somewhere. This Edmund Quincy II proceeded

to settle his new property in English fashion with farms and a small town, which he named Quincy. It was on the edge of that town that Colonel Josiah Quincy, his grandson and my grandfather, built a large house in the year 1770, on an estate of some fair size. He was prominent in the Revolution that some still remember. But wealth and war are not alone the sources of our honor, for we have also exerted ourselves in public life. I was for six years Mayor of Boston and am now President of Harvard College. By no-one more illustrious, I may say, in this whole Commonwealth of Massachusetts, could the illustrious composer have been invited for this summer of his presence in the New World.

But off with you. I know I am not at the center of your interests. I will, however, return.

17 – Going Away (2)

We do not know quite when the Lowell Masons,
with their four children, their nanny Maria, Bobby,
Olwen, their distinguished visitor, and Thankful,
would have traveled the ten miles from Boston to
Quincy, but this would likely have been toward the
end of June. One could imagine that the discovery
of some diary or journal, kept by someone they
visited soon after their arrival in Quincy, would
enable us to narrow down the date, for a meeting
with the composer would surely have been worth
remarking. We might also want to imagine the
preparations going on, calmly supervised by Abigail
– preparations that would have been necessary for
a family embarking on a stay that would likely last
two months, maybe more. A seamstress has been
brought in to mend Abigail's two formal gowns.

The children have been given a small chest, of two cubic feet in capacity, in which to place whatever books, games, and toys they want to have with them. Lowell Mason is handing Bobby a pair of pants that needs pressing. Thankful clips shut a portfolio containing the pages so far finished of the oratorio.

No doubt their host will have sent two or three carriages to Myrtle Street at a set time, and traffic is held up a while as boxes and bags are loaded. Then they all get in, the coachmen knowing to hold doors open for the family, among whom, paying attention to matters of attire, they include the composer and Thankful, but not the servants.

"Do we have everything?"

"Yes, my dear."

"Then off!"

18 – Accommodations

Quincy House was – is – substantial but not enormous, and if all the seven children of Mr. and Mrs. Josiah Quincy III kept rooms there – they ranged in age from twenty to thirty-five – the place would have been full. The earliest map of the town available from, again, the Norman B. Leventhal Map Center, dates from a generation later, 1857, but perhaps not so much had changed; two houses are shown, in the middle of a large parcel of land leading down to the sea, a parcel that by 1894, as evidenced by the next map of the town, had been criss-crossed by streets, this hatching speaking of the family's decline in prosperity after our period.

It is very possible that the surveyors of 1857 ignored, or were unable to examine, the fine detail of what was then still a large estate – and still held by Josiah III, who lived into his nineties. Certainly it is possible, even likely, that Quincy House in 1833 had the advantage, as a real estate agent might put it, of smaller houses and cottages dependent on it: homes for farm and estate workers, guest accommodations. A house and a small cottage could well have been made available for the Lowell Mason party, the house for Lowell and Abigail, with their children and servants, the cottage for the great composer and his helpmeet – not his mouthpiece but his earpiece. The two dwellings need not have been adjacent or even near one another, for surely Mr. Quincy's interest in inviting these people lay indeed in their guest, to whom he would be sure to have his own access, independent of this Mason fellow.

Perhaps there was some tussle between the two wives, Abigail Gregory Mason and Eliza Susan Morton Quincy, to give them names they surely never thought of themselves as bearing at the time. Abigail was of an age with Mrs. Quincy's eldest child, and so the difference of generation was added to that of social ascendancy. Was the wife of the President of Harvard to defer to someone married to a bank clerk? But would she perhaps nevertheless have done so, on the grounds that this person would have some experience in handling the distinguished visitor, would know his needs?

However it came about, the place was arranged. The great composer and his aural assistant have the use of a single-story *cottage orné* just a short walk from the main house, with the Lowell Mason family a little further off. The place is presently used most often by the eldest son of the Quincy family, Josiah IV, but he and his wife and their two infant sons had piled into his old room in the big house for the duration of the great composer's visit. Thus vacated, the cottage would offer the most suitable accommodation, Eliza Susan Quincy judged, because it afforded entirely separate quarters for "the girl." Having heard that their famous guest had the use of a Chickering piano at the Lowell Masons', she responded by having the Quincy Broadwood installed in the cottage.

The important guest and his "ear", as she was called by the Quincys, were shown their accommodations by a young woman, the deputy housekeeper, who, having been told of the gentleman's disability, performed the task as much as she could by means of smiles and gestures, though sometimes she would have to explain something to Thankful. Then or later, Thankful would be able to impart the information to the one she was coming to regard – yes, now that they were in a new environment she could see this – not as a lofty master but rather, the half century and other mountains between them flattened by his dependence, as a friend. The question of how he considered her never arose in her mind. This room, she signed, gives access through the French windows to the garden and the ocean beyond. It catches the morning light. Yes, you can gaze toward your Europe, your home.

When the woman had gone, the great musician sat down – she had left them in what had been furnished as his study – and waved a hand for Thankful to do the same. They smiled at one another. They laughed. And then, the composer having raised a hand, Thankful smacked hers against it, and they laughed even more. This had never happened at Myrtle Street. They were on vacation.

19 – A Letter

(2179) *To ?*

[*Autograph not traced*]
QUINCY, *June 29,* 1833

I write, having a favor to ask of you, for we are now so distant from each other that we can no longer converse together, and, indeed, unhappily, we can seldom write either. You surely realize how much I dislike troubling you. I hope, therefore, that you will forgive me for putting this question to you: Is Dr. Spiecker still in Vienna? I would certainly like to know the truth!

Be graciously indulgent towards me, for so many trying occurrences, succeeding each other so closely, have really almost bewildered me; still I am convinced that the resplendent beauties of Nature here, and the charming environs, will gradually restore my spirits. What happiness I shall feel in wandering among groves and woods, and among trees, and plants, and rocks! No man on earth can love the country as I do! Thickets, trees, and rocks supply the echo man longs for!

For the next concert for the benefit of the Reverend Ursulines I promise to let you have at once an entirely new symphony. That is the least I am sending, but perhaps I shall add something suitable for voices – and since I can now manage to do so, I shall see that the copying does not cost a single farthing.

I shall be here until the end of September.

With kindest regards, your admirer and friend,

20 – Dinner at Quincy (in General)

The arrangements for dinner were probably always the same, the long table covered with linen and lace so that never an inch of its naked oak be seen, the candles enough to substitute for the heavily curtained-off daylight and bring sparkle to the glass and silver, the places set, the servants ready, and yet at the same time always different, on account of which members of the family and which guests were present. The junior Josiah Quincy was rarely there, having business in the city, and his wife Mary Jane would be with him, leaving their two young boys to her mother's care. The senior Josiah Quincy also traveled back and forth, with his wife and whatever number of their four unmarried daughters. Margy, the one married daughter, could well have been off botanizing with her husband, the two of them rarely seen at Quincy. Not so the younger son, Edmund, and his fiancée Lucilla, as well as more distant relations, appearing and disappearing like figures on a clock. As for the Lowell Masons, it might often seem more convenient to them to dine at their own place, with their young children. Sometimes the eternal master and his assistant would be seated alone, still with the candles blazing on so many unused settings.

Thankful had presented a social problem to the hostess. She had to be considered a servant, but it was essential, if the great composer were to be engaged in conversation, that she should have a place where he could see her, and where she could, of course, hear others at the table. Mrs. Quincy had therefore had the servants set up a small table a little way to the left of her husband's place, so that their notable guest, on Mr. Quincy's right, would be able to observe the wretched girl's hand gestures without these being an embarrassment to everyone else. Seeing this, however, the great composer had at once objected and insisted against all possible decorum that Thankful be reseated at the table, across from him and a little to his right.

By this time, of course, the esteemed visitor had for many years been avoiding exactly the sort of social intercourse as now presented itself every evening at Quincy, except on those occasions when he and Thankful were the only ones present, in which case they would keep their hands in their laps and enjoy

their shared silence. He might have wondered how
he could once more participate in polite conversation, such as had not been expected of him in Myrtle
Street, but he found, with some mixture of relief
and weariness, that the rules and gambits came
back to him with uncanny immediacy and accuracy.
He could enlighten Mrs. Quincy on the famous
pastries of the Austrian capital, answer Miss Maria
Sophia Quincy's notably astute questions as to why
he had not written and would not write a concerto
for the violoncello, agree sagely with Mr. Edmund
Quincy on the perils of absolutism, and discuss
with Miss Margy Quincy the nature of fossils. All of
them around the table would have been interested
to learn of his experiences during his voyage
across the ocean, an adventure none of them had
undertaken, nor would undertake, perhaps in wary
consciousness of the elder Mr. Quincy's father,
who had died at sea, breathing his last, so it was
said, within sight of the coast of his beloved
Massachusetts. Their curiosity was surely stanched,
however, when the composer retorted: "My journey
was terrible!"

It was at dinner, most of all, that the composer
had opportunities to regard this little society. There
was, of course, no aristocracy in the republic, no
froth of counts and highnesses, nor was there yet
the colossal wealth of Viennese houses he had
frequented, fragile as that wealth had often turned

out to be. The Quincys would have been rather at the level of court officials and high-ranking civil servants he had known, imitating the manners of means and nobility on a more modest scale. Yet he could detect at once several notable differences. One would be in the general nature of the relationship between the family and its servants, an absence of presumption: of superiority on the one side and deference on the other. Of course, Mr. Quincy could command his butler and not the other way about, but both of them seemed possessed of the knowledge that, besides being master and servant, they were many other things as well. Such an awareness would never have occurred to a Viennese gentleman, and would have been understood by his servant as an interference in the domain of the private. Here, too, there was respect on both sides, and caution. What separated them, though, was not a step, with an above and a below, but a distance, on the same level.

Did this difference from Viennese custom – perhaps one could say from European custom – pertain to the nature of a republic, he might wonder, or was it embedded rather in a difference of religion, between a people for whom individual souls were all equal at the same apex of paramountcy and a Catholic empire, in which admission to the Godhead came by way of a hierarchy of degrees?

He would undoubtedly have felt it, too, within

himself, the ease and familiarity with which he was welcomed by all, of whatever station in life, and even engaged in conversation. In Vienna, he would hardly have needed to be told, it was his genius that gained him access to the higher strata of society, but nothing there could win him acceptance also by the lower. He could count an archduke his friend but not a washerwoman. Here, though he would never have been invited had he not been a person of distinction, what seemed to matter to Mr. Quincy was more fundamental, a kinship of honesty and frankness to be found in this visitor. And it was the same meeting on a human plane that made it possible for a housemaid or a kitchen boy – how impossible this would have been in Austria – to inquire as to his progress on the great work in which everyone seemed to be taking an interest.

And yes, there would be time to go back to the cottage and draft a few more measures before retiring.

21 – Further Concerns

"Does he appear more at ease out there?"

"Hard to say. You see, he has his own place, with the girl. A cottage, some little way from the house and quite separate from where we are being accommodated. I have less access to him than I did here in the city."

"That is unfortunate."

"Not necessarily. He may well, as you were suggesting, feel freer, I would even say looser. Able to get on with things at his own pace."

"Things."

"I mean the oratorio, of course."

"Of which you have still seen nothing?"

"Nothing."

"I do hope he has had occasion to meet Mr. Colburn."

"Whether sketches or a fair copy?"

"Nothing."

"It really is high time we questioned him – challenged him. Gentlemen, we have a performance in little more than four months!"

"I can only counsel patience."

"Patience."

"As before."

22 – The Fourth of July

Cath'rine wheels on the barn
Spinning light fantastic

It pleased him to see these flashes and streaks and whirligigs of colored light reflected in the eyes of the six young boys, their faces all tilted up to the show, as indeed was his, turning now – Thankful tugged on his sleeve – to watch with her the stream of yellow sparks, all falling in a general rise, and then the dark silent moment before the flower burst high up there, and its crack an instant after. She tugged on his sleeve again and threw him a smile, for a second not realizing, in her excitement, that he had heard nothing. But still he smiled back. Perhaps he had never seen such things before; in Vienna, one celebrated with a Mass. But here it was a custom, as his host had told him, adding that this year he had asked for an exceptional performance to honor the coming-of-age of his youngest daughter, Miss Anna, whose birthday they had marked a week before with

a bottle of champagne served by the faltering butler
into so many glasses that the sip was almost flat by
the time it reached one's lips. Abstemiousness then
had now been replaced by lavish splendor.

> *Slowly the candle burns*
> *Into eternity*

But this Roman one could not go on forever
launching its bombs to ascend three or four feet
and there go on blazing, as if in an effort against
the gravity taking hold of them: red, orange-yellow,
blue-green. No doubt the colors shone from his own
eyes, too, which would throw back light with no less
happy immediacy, though clouded within. Yes, the
display made children of them all. Magic and magnificence had only this to say: Look! Look! Look!
And music?

> *Sparkling and bright is the light of Independence*

And in the rush and the gush of the volcano,
ejecting jagged splinters of white light from within
yellow flame, could he sense himself in the heat of
composition, casting through ideas nearly all of
which would blaze and die? No, it was not true that
the adults here were recovering the innocent glee
of childhood. It was all fake, created by a powder
concealed in brightly colored packaging labeled

with a name invented to stimulate an astonishment as artificial as the fear: "Vesuvius," "Minefield," "Crimson Blazer," "Shooting Stars." They knew better. They knew more. What, after all, was this sparkling festival? Washington. Jefferson. Of course he was familiar with these names; their bearers were among the pioneers of human freedom. They were put on earth to realize what Schiller, with the wide-eyed optimism of youth, had projected. But youth and childhood, they do not tarry. There comes the firm, unyielding grip of experience. He had tried to bring the experience of experience to the youth-fulness of youth. *Alle Menschen werden Brüder. Alle Menschen, alle Menschen.* Because he thought there was a place on earth where this music would be felt to exist in the present tense. Was that it? Not in France, where Revolution had brought Terror, Bureaucracy, Empire, and now a succession of the old king's brothers back on the righted, benighted throne. But here. Where, however, was the spirit of Washington and Jefferson in this contrived jollifi-cation, which covered – the analogy with the Mass was just – a lack of belief in what it pretended to celebrate? *O Freunde, nicht diese Töne.*

Over there they flare and burst asunder

There is no way of knowing now if he would have visited the granite quarries at Quincy, about three miles distant from Quincy House. Excursions on foot are to be presumed; they had been a customary part of his summer regimen for decades. It is likely he would very often take his walk in the company of his host, for the two men were of an age – a year and seven weeks separated them – and perhaps equal in stamina, though whether both remained capable of a round trip of six or seven miles is a moot point. An expedition by carriage would, of course, have been possible. But we have no idea how Josiah Quincy viewed this relatively new enterprise in the town that was, by its name, his. Neither in the quarries nor in the horse-drawn railroad that linked them to the river did he have any financial stake, but perhaps that need not have dissuaded him from making this nearby example of modern industry the object of a tour. Who can say? The railroad itself was a spectacle, a three-mile stretch plus a hundred-yard incline rising at one-in-four. Their esteemed visitor could have seen nothing like it, for there were no horsecar tramways in Vienna until 1840. Then there were the quarries themselves: cliffs diving down as the stone was extracted, levels on which men hammered and chiseled and drove in wedges to separate the hard blue rock in slabs and blocks, in all that heat, their efforts adding to the heat. Sweat. Sweat mixed with the rough dust and gravel. Their skin scraped and scoured, even through a shirt, salt sweat stinging the grazes.

This he could have observed, peering down. *Alle Menschen werden Brüder.* Here were the hauliers, eight of them heaving on ropes to pull a block to where it could be loaded on to a cart, one wiping a cut hand across his forehead, another leaning on a shovel gasping, and the clank and grind of metal tools on the stone, and the horses waiting and dragging, and all of it purposeful, like the insides of a clock, all of it operating as of itself, because the operators are elsewhere. And the squared-off lumps of rock go off, trundling along the railroad – more noise – to build the façades of banks in the city. Granite for strength, granite for solidity, granite for longevity. Put your trust in us. We have been here forever. Blocks tucked in tight. No sweat.

The fizz of the fuse and we know what's to come

But if he was there, staring down the hewn rockfaces into the pit, would he have thought thus? Could he have? Vienna was a city of imperial rule, of highly concentrated wealth, of police spies, of near-poverty and servitude for the vast mass of the population. There were banks there, too, and palaces, the palaces of noblemen on whom he had depended for his freedom.

It's a tiny explosion and very soon gone

The brightness again on these children's faces, fading. For them, the Revolution is all in the past, before even their parents' time, a topic to be studied in history class. Soon, Taps would have been played over the last veteran of Washington's Continental Army. The brightness fading. To be relit? Was that the message of the evening's entertainment?

There might be an old servant to tell the notable visitor of the rebellion that took place here in Massachusetts, but in the western part of the state, in 1786-7, a rebellion of small farmers against the inequitable economic conditions of the young republic – a rebellion condoned by Jefferson, if from afar, from Paris, as necessary to the continuing health even of a liberated republic. Would this go on happening, a perpetual rhythm of uprisings that, though they might be suppressed, would prompt change in the means and purposes of government, and perhaps even of greater revolts that would install a whole new manner of government, required by some shift in society or in general expectations, blaze after blaze? Or was all this fire and light a pageant that would, in commemorating, fix?

And our spirits will soar like a rocket in flight

There were twenty-four of them, set off one after another.

23 – A Walk

"Another wonderful day," the elder Josiah would say, knowing that the great composer, striding beside him, would know nothing of what he said, for they did not take Thankful with them on these outings, yet feeling it necessary to keep up conversation, if a soliloquy might be considered such, partly because to walk along in silence would have seemed to him dismal and unfriendly, but perhaps also for other reasons. "I cannot tell you how much I enjoy these perambulations of ours, to get away from the house and all that, to observe the wheat ripening, to hear the birds – in a word, to breathe – but also, of course, and most of all, for the pleasure of your company, my dear friend, as I hope I may call you." Every time, he would insert this phrase. "Otherwise I could be taking this walk by myself, which somehow I never do. Not alone, no, for it seems to me essential to the nature of a walk that it be shared. The purpose of a walk is to be released from oneself, and walking alone one is, rather, plunged into one's own thoughts, so that a rose opening in a hedge, or a maple reddening, or even the bright whistle of a lark will all go unnoticed beneath the churning struggle to formulate a difficult letter, or the worrying how to console a heartbroken daughter, to speak only of such mental squalls. With another beside one, however, one's eyes are focused outward, not turned within, into the shapeless gloom. I hope you agree with me. I feel sure you do. We walk in the daylight, we two, not the shadows. And good day to you, Mr. Appleton. Thank you, she is well. That was my neighbor Appleton. He has land to the north-west of here – better land than mine, it must be said, but he has to make his living from it. Josiah and Edmund, my sons, are constantly trying to persuade me to drain these marshes, which they tell me could subsequently be treated with lime and converted into fine pasture. We might even grow corn here, they say, with some hedges to protect us from the wind. But I will leave that for Josiah to attend to. I am satisfied with the place as it is, to view it as I did more than half a century ago, when I walked these paths with my grandfather. Moreover, my friend, and I feel quite sure you will agree with me on this point, unspoiled Nature gives us a fairer prospect than does agriculture. Rather the irregular geometry of the beneficent goddess than rectangular fields and rows of plantings. I know you are with me. Besides, what would become of my warblers? Listen. Oh, pray forgive me. But if only you could, my dear friend. Mind the ditch there. What a symphony they treat us to! Oh, and if only such music could be given out by the instruments of an orchestra, presenting us with a composition from the hand of Nature herself – and, yes, incorporating the shrieks of these gulls, too! How might we portray them? With clarinets, played in some raw fashion, as if by beginners? But perhaps my sense of humor is not so very apt, my dear friend. I must apologize. But with you, walking here beside me, I feel I can say whatever comes into my head, however inappropriate. I let go my guard. At least, up to a point I do so. We all have these secret rooms in our souls that we will not open to anyone, not to our wives or husbands, not to our closest friend or most trusted ally. Yes, I fear we all keep ourselves strangers. Otherwise any kind of social life would be quite impossible. Otherwise it would be quite impossible for me to be out here with you now, which I so much enjoy, allowing my thoughts to range, but only up to a certain point. Not beyond. If we take a right here we could descend gently to the beach. Which reminds me of another of Josiah's and Edmund's plans, that we set up a sea-bathing establishment here. A bathhouse. Guest rooms. But let them proceed with this, too, when it is their turn. Take care: there's a little step just around the corner. In my opinion, the sea should be left the resort of fishes and crabs, and of fishermen who will bring these things to our table. And yes, I should have mentioned this earlier, that we will have three visitors this evening whom I am sure you will enjoy meeting. Careful again. And from here we have a view of the ocean and the whole length of the strand. Can you imagine this filled with people frolicking in the waves in their disgusting bathing costumes? We can go on down. Yes, three visitors. One is a cousin of mine, and I believe she brings one of her granddaughters with her as a traveling companion. She is a widow. My cousin, I mean. Her late husband, Dr. Hill, was in his maturer years our city's Postmaster, having served in his youth in the navy, I believe as a surgeon. A curious career, but a very fine and interesting man. Gone now, alas, as I say. Wushówunan. Their marriage was to all appearances extremely happy, and I believe truly was so. Cousin Hannah was, of course, powerfully stricken with grief when her husband was taken from us three years ago, but I sense she was filled with so much calm joy, through the many years they had together, that this now steadies her in her mourning. You will find her solemn but by no means woeful. And she knows a good deal more of music than I do – as of most things. She is, indeed, a very remarkable woman, of powerful intellect and sweeping imagination, but all in a person so warm and engaging. One of my professors refers to her

supper parties as 'colloquia by candlelight.' And yes,
I hope she will play for us. Or that her granddaughter
will. I feel I should apologize to you again that most
of my own offspring so lack facility in your art. Anna,
of course, is the exception. Edmund has a splendid
voice, but suffers from embarrassment when he is
called upon to make use of it in public. That is why
we have been able to offer you so little in the way of
musicales, but then –. The seeds of grasses I find
endlessly fascinating. Note the delicacy of these,
weighing down the stem that supports them, so that
it describes a graceful curve. Or am I still talking
about my children? There are so many of them, and
yet how few, the ground here being already packed
with such a congregation, will be able to germinate,
spring forth, and in due time become graceful
stems with seeds of their own. That signal I think
will be the ferry from Plymouth. I am not sure I can
quite make out which of all these ships it must be.
Of course, it is satisfying to see the evidence of how
well our nation thrives, but I used sometimes to
come here very early of a summer's morning in order
to see the sea stretch out empty, soundless. One can
feel oneself alone in all the world at such a time, with
only the birds for company, alone at a point when all
of human history has passed, or before it has begun.
Perhaps we could do that, you and I, before you
leave us. I would like that, to be walking with you in
eternal silence."

24 – What Remains

Even the whereabouts of the cottage at Quincy occupied by the composer and his – perhaps the word should indeed be "amanuensis," as hands, after all, were what Thankful was using – are unknown, and there are no drawings of it, so that we have very little information as to its layout. Only a few references in Quincy family letters and journals offer some clue, suggesting two interior doors, to right and left, immediately inside the entrance, each door giving access to two or three rooms quite separate from those entered through the other, with no connection between the two suites, as it were – a kind of semi-detached arrangement. There are reports that the roof was thatched in the English manner, but then Maria Quincy, in her journal, records having been woken in the night by a heavy slate falling. In any event, nothing of the structure is to be seen, and visitors nowadays to Quincy House will be disappointed if they go in expectation of any sign at all that the composer was there. Restoration of the decor and furnishings began with Abigail Quincy, the elder Josiah's second daughter (Maria was his third), whose work pointed her successors toward maintaining, or reinstating, the domestic conditions of the later nineteenth century, several decades, therefore, after the period that concerns us. There might be a receipt from S. H. Parker of Boston, who supplied and shipped the Broadwood, but no trace exists of the instrument itself. Of almost nothing in the house may it be said with any uncertainty that it was in place when the great composer was visiting, still less that he might have used it.

To move outside the house, no more to be seen is the Quincy pinetum, or the carousel of irises arranged in wedges of thirty degrees to flower in clockwise order, or the lime avenues of the further park, or the path through the wilderness of sedge, or the climb down to the beach, or the hut the young male Quincys would use when going down in the afternoons to plunge into the ocean.

As to what happened here that summer of 1833, however, there can be no doubt but that a substantial portion of the Boston oratorio was achieved during the two months or so the composer spent at Quincy. It is true there is no mention of the work in the composer's surviving correspondence from Quincy, except possibly where he refers to "a work of some importance for voices" in a letter to an unknown friend in Vienna written very early in the period. (As has often been pointed out, the composer does not specify that this is a piece on which he is currently engaged; it could be an old work, or one he was merely planning.) Nor, of course, was it his practice to inscribe dates on his drafts or sketches, or on the fair copy he would be putting together as numbers found their final or near-final shape. However, the autograph materials appear to have included three *cartes de visite* (a possible fourth is questionable) listed in an 1877 inventory of the Brunswick court library but not subsequently seen. The names and addresses on these, recorded not in the inventory but in a daybook kept by a visitor to the library around the same time, may be found in other Quincy documents, which strongly suggests they were left with the composer by local admirers. On the reverse of each card, the composer sketched themes, which happily the visitor copied into her daybook, and which have been identified, not entirely uncontroversially, as having been incorporated into the final work. A lingering tradition has it that most of the oratorio, in its final form, was composed or refashioned during the Quincy period, but it is difficult to trace the origins of this belief, given the paucity of documentary evidence. It is just about possible that the composer could, in so few weeks, have created a work of such a size and complexity, but the immediacy would have been uncommon for him at any time and would seem to require some explanation. As it stands, we can only wait for papers relating to the work – musical drafts, letters, memoranda – to come to light, whether at Quincy House or elsewhere.

25 – Dinner at Quincy (in Particular)

On the evening in question there would have been fourteen around the table, with Cousin Hannah, Mrs. Hill, seated between the senior Mr. Quincy, to her left, and the composer. At first, Mrs. Hill could well have felt it awkward to communicate through Thankful, to say something and then experience the inevitable delay for the relaying of it to be completed so that the response could then come. Besides, she had not seen her cousin Josiah in a while, and, being nine years older, had always had a quasi-maternal interest in his affairs, an interest that, given its warmth, he could not but welcome. As the evening proceeded, however, and as she came to realize, once again, that nothing much was going to change in Josiah's dealings with the world, or its with him, and as she got used to Thankful's silent interventions and could feel herself to be conversing with the great composer directly, she found herself spending more and more time turned to her right.

"I must say," said Mrs. Hill, "the pork is exceptionally fine."

"I think it is excellent," said the composer.

"Often one finds," Mrs. Hill went on, though rapidly realizing she was pursuing the point unnecessarily and even wastefully, and all the time the item under discussion was getting colder, while the gentleman to whom she was speaking held his fork unmoving, "that a roast pork will be dry and lacking in flavor, and most of all at this time of the year."

She stopped, and returned to the substance in question. Keeping the composer in view through a corner of her eye, she observed him also now chewing, and seemingly unlikely to want to add anything further to the topic. Having swallowed, however, he turned, and so did she, so that they now faced each other, for the first time in the evening.

"I need not assure you of my sympathy," he said, and nodded in the direction of the portrait locket she wore at her right breast, with two short lengths of black ribbon hanging from it, "with your misfortune."

He kept his eyes on her, no doubt knowing he would not need Thankful's help, as she replied: "Thank you."

As she spoke those words, she felt as if she had never uttered them before. They both went back to the pork and the corn mash.

"Your children must really be a great comfort to you," said the composer, this time without looking up from his plate.

"Oh, indeed they are, and certainly so is my dear, dear Mary" – and here she would have nodded down the table to a young woman of nineteen who had just lifted her head in laughter while keeping her eyes on the older man next to her, further down, who certainly was keeping his eyes on her – "down there talking to that gentleman from Russia. She is my dear Tommy's daughter, and was my only grandchild until little Billy arrived, three months ago."

The composer misunderstood Thankful's transmission here, construing Mrs. Hill as speaking of this Mary as her daughter, not her granddaughter. Though he had returned his gaze to his plate, his response was somewhat vehement. "Generally speaking," he said, "Russians and Livonians are windbags and braggarts."

Mrs. Hill was not entirely sure where Livonia was, but she let that pass. What she understood from the remark – and who is to say whether she was right or wrong? – was that her granddaughter's charms had not been lost on the great composer.

"Mary," she said, "is a very capable child. She has developed quite an interest in the science of mathematics."

"Educate your daughter carefully," the composer responded, his voice still stern, "that she may make a good wife."

Mrs. Hill took a hard breath and was about to offer some correction, perhaps some rejoinder (unless she was only stifling a sneeze), but decided instead to close the topic.

"Thank you," she said. "I shall bear that in mind."

By now the raspberry ice would have been served, and for a while they paid it all their attention. Then it was Mrs. Hill who reinitiated conversation.

"I hope you have been enjoying your visit to our New World." And instantly she regretted having issued such a banality, betraying the intimacy and trust the composer had so immediately offered. She need not have feared, however, for the composer replied with a confidence.

"I am now leading a slightly more pleasant life," he said, "for I am mixing more with my fellow creatures," at which he simultaneously smiled at her and gestured across the table to Thankful.

"Indeed," said Mrs. Hill, "I can imagine that your life as a composer is very much solitary."

"I am entirely devoted to my Muses," the composer replied, "as I always have been; and in this alone do I find the joy of my life."

Mrs. Hill noted that word "alone" (*allein*) and felt it perhaps hinted at a truth the composer was not prepared to admit, or perhaps covertly was admitting. She would remember this, but not pursue it at the moment.

"You have been in attendance on your Muses" – her tone was serious – "while here in Massachusetts?" Everyone knew that this was so, but she was not thinking of everyone just now.

"I hope yet to usher some great works into the world," the composer responded, "and then to close my earthly career like an old child somewhere among good people." And again he cast her a smile.

"And among those great works," Mrs. Hill went on, "will be the oratorio for our Society here in Boston?"

The composer nodded, but added: "I am also composing a new string quartet."

Mrs. Hill was struck with surprise and delight. "Oh my goodness," she said, "what a thing. A string quartet in your head right now, as we sit here. A string quartet by you at Quincy."

"I know no more charming enjoyment in the country," the composer continued, "than quartet music."

Mrs. Hill waited a while before going on with the conversation. The raspberry ice, to be sure, also merited some notice. But was the great composer playing with her? Could he really be classing chamber music – chamber music as he conceived and practiced it – as rural entertainment? Perhaps he was testing her out.

"I wonder at your saying so," she said. "To me, even your very first achievements in this genre – I would cite the extraordinary finale to the quartet in B flat you placed last in your Opus 18 collection, or even the string trios from before that – are far beyond charming. The word does not even come to one's mind in their context without it jars. Nor is there question of their being right for any particular audience or circumstance; rather the audience must be right for them."

The composer said nothing.

"I really have not the nimbleness and strength in my fingers any more," Mrs. Hill went on, "but in earlier times I was known to play through your quartets and trios at the keyboard."

This was all pushing at the limits of what could be conveyed by signs, but Thankful was doing her utmost to convey nuance. As for the composer, he sometimes felt, as now, that he hardly needed her hand gestures, could read the meaning in her face.

They finished their ices. Mrs. Hill did not catch some announcement Cousin Josiah made, at which two or three of the company got up from the table.

"Besides," she continued, linking them back to where they had been before, linking them back together, "the country has its own charms, not to be found in town. Walking, for example."

The composer turned to her with a sudden excitement that was almost alarming. "If possible come to me tomorrow," he said. "I leave it to you to fix the time. If you could make it about noon, that would suit me best."

"Then about noon," she found herself saying, before rising as if drawn up by some other power. She had not offered her hand, but the composer took it and kissed it as he, too, got up from his chair. Seeing this, Thankful also rose. A kind of suspension hovered, with the three of them standing and looking at one another.

Mrs. Hill turned and left.

26 – Growing Concerns

"You have heard nothing from Mason?"

"His sons have been bathing daily and have made a pet of a starfish."

"I mean nothing about the oratorio?"

"My dear friend, I would have told you at once."

"Of course. Forgive me, but the silence, the lack of information, is beginning to wear me down."

"I understand, I understand. But the responsibility is one we all share."

"What can we do?"

"I have sent a letter to Mason, entreating him to press for some clear indication of when the parts for the soloists will be ready and when we may expect to see the finished score."

"You think he will do this? You think he *can* do this?"

"What other option do we have?"

"We could send Mr. Ballou."

"I think not."

"We could change the program."

"Has anything been heard of Mr. Colburn's participation?"

"We could. We could indeed. We may have to. But I very much hope – indeed, I have every confidence – that the composition will be completed in time, and we will be able to go ahead as planned. We have summoned the genius of the age to the New World. Have we done so for nothing? No, no. That cannot be the story. The world is waiting for this great work, and the world will be satisfied."

27 – An Intervention

Sorry, but we have to stop you there. You keep teasing us with this "great work" while offering as little information about it as you can get away with. Like these characters who are presumably from the Handel and Haydn Society, perhaps Richardson, Chickering and some other, we are being left in the dark. We know, yes, that this is an oratorio he is supposed to be writing, this "great composer," as you archly call him, or "distinguished visitor," or whatever else to avoid giving him his name, which of course we all know, which you have had to divulge here and there, for the purposes of your story. Yes, what exactly are the purposes of your story? Do you want to tell us that? Or is that not part of your plan? If there is a plan.

You tell us how – for God's sake, let's use the name – Beethoven was approached by the Handel and Haydn Society of Boston, through the U. S. consul in Vienna, to compose an oratorio to a text in English, and we believe you. You give us a footnote to confirm the fact. From that, you go on to launch the fiction that Beethoven did not die on March 26, 1827, a date on which all reference works agree, but lived on several years more, enough to travel to Boston in 1833 to complete the oratorio and bring it to performance, and yes, we go along for the ride.

We are not here now to dispute the virtues of fiction. Let's take that matter as read, can we? What we do dispute, however, is your right to hold back information.

You fill this book with information. As if to taunt us, you tell us all kinds of things we do not need to know, such as the names and ages and trades of other passengers (the shipboard septet – oh, please) on the vessel that could have conveyed the "great composer" to Boston. Remember that one? And we know where you find all these annoyingly irrelevant details. You even admit as much: on the Internet. So what?

We have come this far largely in silence. We have played the game. We have done our part. But we cannot go on keeping quiet when you continue to withhold what we most want to know, which is not the facts of the matter but the fiction. Is Beethoven really stalling? If so, why? Or has he in fact (as it were) almost finished the score? Or has he hit a block? Most of all, what is the supposed subject of this supposed oratorio? You must know. We have been patient long enough. Over to you. Get on with it.

28 – A Midday Meeting

The following morning the great composer was at his desk in the Quincy cottage at first light. Yes, the work had been giving him difficulties, partly on account of Mr. Ballou's text, but also, and more importantly, because he wanted to find a whole new form and voice for the oratorio as a genre. The very name of the institution that had commissioned the piece – the Handel and Haydn Society – advertised exactly the constraint he felt, almost as a cramp in his shoulders. *Judas Maccabeus. The Creation.* These were magnificent achievements: strong steps in the progress of music and, what counted for more, moral examples of humanity in wholesome contract with the Divine, and vice versa, the terms of that contract written in song to be read by the soul. But both music and morality could be caught only in motion, in advance, and oratorio, of all types of composition, most lacked the necessary agility. Its inclination was to stiffen – you felt that in Haydn; you felt it in Handel. You certainly felt it in his own work, *Christ on the Mount of Olives*. But that was thirty years ago. Now, he believed, after his opera *Der Sturm*, he was ready to make oratorio, too, bend and spring. He felt the sense of what he was after, just a little ahead of him. The problem was how to bring it near – or reach out and grasp it. The problem was to know exactly what it was. A work of art had to be beautiful, of course, but beautiful in a new way. It had to be new, but new in a beautiful way. A kind of pincer operation was required, to take hold of something that might appear to exist already – fully formed, even sounding – but that would come into existence only very slowly, quarter-note by quarter-note, in the act of composition. And even that act would have to be newly founded, to seize its particular prey. Now both were nearer, the oratorio and the strategy to achieve it.

Poor Ballou, of course, had written a crusted libretto that Handel a century ago would have thought outmoded. But, after all, that need not matter. He had begun to transpose lines, with Thankful's help, weave words from an aria into a chorus, for instance, release the air locked in Ballou's words. Still, though, there was resistance. Some of what he had written – perhaps everything he had brought with him from Vienna – would have to be discarded, and yet there was much he felt he could adapt to the kind of muscular stream he now felt himself approaching, or being approached by. Another step would have him there. But in which direction was it to be found?

Pink light hit the faint haze in the room, but he was bent over the pages on his desk.

Two hours passed before Thankful was up, two hours of good work. This was no time to stop. When he saw her come into the room, he bellowed a greeting and the request to be brought some breakfast where he was. That was good news. He was working, working well. One result of being involved in every conversation the great man had was that she was not only his ear but his diary, and when she came in with the tray, she put it down to remind him of the appointment he had made with Mrs. Hill. He was aware. Let her come. Bring her in as soon as she arrived.

Meanwhile, he continued to write. Can we imagine what might have been involved, what processes, mental and physical? He might have had on his desk a draft of the whole oratorio as so far completed, but perhaps he worked with just the immediate sequence to hand. In either case, the music was probably unorchestrated as yet, the notation showing the vocal parts in detail, both solo and choral, with a waft of incompletely indicated accompaniment. There would have been a sketchbook on that desktop, too, and perhaps loose sheets transcribing material to be worked up and worked in. Fresh paper from Peter Jones. Ink. A pen. A knife. Disorder would fit the stereotype: sheets sliding to the floor, the composer in a rage over a lost page. But perhaps his working habits were contrariwise neat. He might have been rushing to set down ideas as they came rushing into his mind. But the rapid hand could have been attached to a body otherwise quiet and calm. We have no idea.

There was a knock at the door, which of course would not have interrupted him. Thankful had to let the lady into the cottage, then go in to his study and enter his field of vision to let him know his visitor had come.

It would not have taken Mrs. Hill very long to observe the mass of papers, and the composer perhaps still with pen in hand as he got up from his chair.

"My dear sir," she would have to say, "I fear my arrival is inopportune. You are evidently in the ecstasy of composition. I should never have come. Indeed, I should never have come."

From watching Thankful's hands, the composer slowly turned his head to look at Mrs. Hill with sadness in his eyes.

"Am I not your true friend?" he said. "It does me good to revive the old feelings of friendship." Then he clapped his hands and added: "Now no more, my dear sweet friend."

Knowing that the composer was inclined to forget the courtesies, Thankful motioned Mrs. Hill to take a seat. She herself remained standing, as was her custom.

"Meanwhile," the composer began again, "I have been composing a good deal."

"That is very good to hear," said Mrs. Hill.

Then, entirely to her surprise, the composer beckoned her to pull up her chair alongside his, at the same time catching Thankful's eye and signing: "Please have the chocolate prepared."

While Thankful was out of the room, the composer cleared space on the desk and brought a pile of folios – his fair copy – to the fore.

"You will probably be able to read my manuscript," he said.

Mrs. Hill almost certainly realized at once it would have been rare for him to take anyone into his creative confidence, especially where a major work in progress was concerned, but she may not have realized quite how rare. She would have suspected immediately – too immediately to be astonished – that she was to be introduced to the Boston oratorio, and it would not have taken her long to recognize that this was so, and even to form in her mind some impression of a choir and orchestra in severe flood.

The music was plunging and rearing up through shadows like a ship on a strong sea in a thunderstorm, but all a little in slow motion. She nodded to the composer to reveal the next page.

At Thankful's return, she was able to speak, and, hardly knowing what to say first, came out with: "This treatment of the submediant is extraordinarily powerful."

"As the wind often does," said the composer, "so do harmonies whirl round me, and so do things often whirl about too in my mind."

"I feel the anxiety here, the desperation," said Mrs. Hill, speaking immediately of her response, not seeking to please the composer, for she knew herself to be with him on a level of openness innocent of contrivance.

It was soon evident that this was his sense of their relationship, too, that there was no need for idle politeness, for he abruptly replied: "Emotion suits women only." And then, as if hearing the harshness in his words, he went on: "Forgive me, music ought to strike fire from the soul of a man."

"I did not realize," said Mrs. Hill softly (and who knows how Thankful would have conveyed matters of tone?), "that our souls must be so very far apart, as woman and man."

Thankful could well have started to feel a little awkward in her presence at this point.

The composer, whose eyes had been on his

manuscript, raised them to those of the person beside him. "The sole real good," he said, "is some bright kindly spirit to sympathize with us, whom we thoroughly comprehend, and from whom we need not hide our thoughts."

Mrs. Hill smiled and returned to inspecting the manuscript, turning its pages now with her own hand.

"This seems to be a fugue, if of an original kind, but why do you do this, here?" she asked.

"Perhaps it was a mistake," the composer replied. "I remember that when writing it down I made one or two mistakes but afterwards forgot all about them."

"I should like to have your opinion about this," he continued, pointing to a measure a little later on the same page. "I am no longer able to obey the rule which I imposed upon myself."

"Nor should you, my dear friend," Mrs. Hill responded. There are occasions when a surprise is necessary – something wholly unexpected – and even welcome."

"Between ourselves," said the composer, again looking up from the manuscript toward his visitor, "the best thing of all is a combination of the surprising and the beautiful."

"In creating which marriages," said Mrs. Hill, instantly regretting her choice of that word, "you are unequaled."

She quickly returned to the great work before her and turned a few pages in silence.

"I think that it will interest the musical public," said the composer.

"Beyond question," said Mrs. Hill, continuing her reading. "This use of the two bassoons," she went on, "well, I have never heard anything like it."

"Usually," the composer replied, "I have to wait for other people to tell me when I have new ideas, because I never know this myself."

"Let me tell you –," began Mrs. Hill.

"Let me tell *you*," the composer interrupted, "that there are still quite enough blunders. I have truly many difficulties to face."

They were both silent a few moments, and then the composer spoke again. "There is still time," he said.

Mrs. Hill considered it would not be productive to continue this line of conversation, and she returned to perusing the score.

As she did so, the composer laughed. "I don't know what it is all about," he said, which could hardly fail to prompt some comment from Mrs. Hill.

"Here," she said, her finger on a measure, "the way this aria for a low soprano voice is written.... How could you have come up with such a glorious melody, and so rich a setting for it?"

The composer hesitated. "A more difficult question could not be put to me," he said, " – and I prefer to leave it unanswered, rather than – to answer it *too truthfully.*"

Once again he looked at Mrs. Hill directly.

"I should be going," she said. "I have taken up too much of your time already." She rose. "Thank you for the chocolate and" – she glanced down at the score – "for this."

The composer did not attempt to detain her.

"If possible," he said, "come to me tomorrow."

"I will."

"I shall tell you more tomorrow."

"At the same time?"

The composer nodded.

"I have done my part," he said, "and on this score" – he smiled, playing with words, as people do with the curios of a foreign vocabulary – "I do not dread appearing before the Highest of all Judges."

"You are achieving a wonder for the ages," said Mrs. Hill, "and on a subject only you could have treated."

Yes, go on. Go on, we say.

"By the way," said the composer, "please do not let anybody know a word of this."

But no: Go on. Go on, either one of you. Tell us.

Mrs. Hill smiled and nodded, but he needed her to confirm her concurrence.

No. Go on.

"Please keep this a secret," he repeated, more emphatically.

Stop this. Go on.

Go on.

"I will," said Mrs. Hill. "Of course I will. It shall not pass my lips."

No. Let it pass them. Go on. Go on.

"This great subject," she said, "so befitting you."

Yes. Right. Go on now.

"The sufferings and the patience of Job."

29 – A Précis

Said GOD to DIS: Look at THIS MAN, how he is just.

Said DIS to GOD: You think THIS MAN is just just for your sake? No. It's a quid pro quo. Trust me. Let him down, down he'll go.

Said GOD to DIS: Do what you must. But spare THIS MAN.

All his stock, each ox, ass, sheep, seized, burned, gone. His ten kids crushed to death.

THIS MAN blessed God.

Said GOD to DIS: Look at THIS MAN, how he still stands.

Said DIS to GOD: Now let me at him, down he'll go.

Said GOD to DIS: Do what you must. But spare his life.

Boils boiled his skin. He scraped his scabs. Said his wife: See what you get? Curse GOD and die.

THIS MAN stayed true.

Three friends came. Said not a word.

THIS MAN said: May the day on which my birth fell fall, time close on it like oil.

Said friend one: So good you were, you would shame GOD. That was your sin.

THIS MAN said: I asked no gift. Now I ask death.

Said friend two: GOD does not err. You must have done wrong.

THIS MAN said: GOD set the stars. His ways are not ours. Try to do right, you walk in the dark.

Said friend three: GOD is not bound. He does what he will.

THIS MAN said: I know all you know. Our time is brief.

Said friend one: Your words are your fault.

THIS MAN said: Go, false friends. I break. You break me more.

Said friend two: Be still. Close your mouth.

THIS MAN said: I speak out my grief, to which you add.

Said friend three: The bad come to no good.

THIS MAN said: No, the bad thrive. Don't waste your breath.

Said friend one: You must have done wrong. You must have done wrong.

THIS MAN said: If I knew where GOD was, I'd plead my cause.

Said friend two: GOD sees it all. None can do right.

THIS MAN said: Dead things form in your mouths.

And THIS MAN said: Though I am lost to GOD, GOD is not lost to me.

And THIS MAN said: To be wise is more than gold.

And THIS MAN said: If I could be as I was.

And THIS MAN said: And not as I am.

And THIS MAN said: GOD has dealt thus.

And THIS MAN said: I played by the rules.

Three friends stood. Said not a word.

One man more spoke: I heard all you said, all three
of you. Now hear what I say, to THIS MAN.

Speak back to GOD? You are a fool.

Can you make a cloud? Can you let fall snow?

Then GOD was heard, his voice a wind whirled.

GOD said: Where were you, when I made the
world?

Where were you, when I made all time?

Where were you, when I made death?

Can you pull down stars?

Can you count rain drops?

Can you change what I do?

Was it you made the horse strong?

Was it you made the hawk fly?

Was it you made the hoar frost?

Fear me.

Fear me.

And THIS MAN said: My hand's on my mouth. I speak
no more.

Go great as you are.

Should I fish for a whale?

Should I hold it fast?

Go great as you are.

Then GOD spoke to the friends: You have me wrong.
THIS MAN has me right.

 Give praise to me, by way of him.

And GOD spoke to THIS MAN: I give you back
             all you had had
             and yet still more.
             So let it end.

30 – In Search of Evidence

It has long been supposed that the composer made no significant advance on the score of his oratorio during the weeks between his arrival in Boston, in May of 1833, and his departure for Quincy at the end of June. Of course, this assertion could easily be thrown into doubt were there to be found, say, a cache of sketch pages written on paper that could not have been acquired other than in Boston, inscribed with ink that would point to a Boston supplier or manufacturer. Even this, though, would not definitively prove such sketches were made at Myrtle Street, for the composer could very well have taken paper and ink with him to Quincy.

Of possible pertinence to the question is the undisputed fact that Miss Anna Cabot Lowell Quincy, writing in her journal of the same year, uses a dark green ink of a quite unusual composition, and so if any manuscript relating to the oratorio were to be discovered written out in this same ink, then the theory that much – perhaps most – of the task of composition was fulfilled at Quincy would gain manifest support. Caution would, nevertheless, be advisable. The so-called "AQ ink" may have been more widely available than supporters of the Quincy theory are inclined to suppose. To clarify the point, it would be necessary to examine and analyze written materials – letters, journals, invoices, receipts – from a wide variety of sources in and around Boston written close to the time in question, a task that would be exceedingly laborious and might not lead to any firm conclusion.

Even if it could be proven with greater assurance that the composer suddenly began to work so much more productively on the oratorio soon after he had decamped with the Lowell Masons to Quincy, there would be no way of knowing for sure, of course, what prompted this renewal of creative energy or confidence. Perhaps there was a compositional problem that, with the passing of time or the move to a new environment, he found he could solve, and that in solving he effectively obliterated, to leave no trace. Perhaps, after a period of frustration, he finally decided to deal more freely with Hosea Ballou's libretto, which is known to us only in its final form, so that there remains no indication of how the wording might have been changed and adapted during the course of the oratorio's composition. Perhaps the impetus came from outside, from the increasing importunity of those grandees of the Handel and Haydn Society with whom the composer was in communication, Mason included.

Our efforts to reconstruct the compositional process will, here and there, have their limits.

31 – Another Midday Meeting

Another midday came – it could have been the following day, or it could have been a little later, when these meetings at the cottage at twelve had become something of a routine, a routine that for Mrs. Hill had matured from excitement to a steadier pleasure, not unmixed at times with confusion and even distress that she could not quite grasp what the composer was asking of her, or how to answer his questions and demands – and Mrs. Hill was there again. It was all as it always was: being let in by Thankful and taken into the composer's study, marveling at what he had achieved since the last visit, which might have been only the day before, being brought a cup of chocolate, and beginning their discussion.

Now and again, not often, there might be some conversation between them on other topics, such as food, or health, and in such a case the composer might have declared: "Since yesterday I have only taken some soup, and a couple of eggs, and drank nothing but water."

A reference to "potato purée" would be another possibility. And Mrs. Hill would be properly sympathetic, or amused. At first, she found such digressions tiresome and unwelcome; she was in the presence of a great artist and did not want to know about, did not want to imagine, his everyday life and his bodily needs, his existence as a creature like herself. Artists should not speak of potato purée. Very soon, however, she came to enjoy how the world-renowned composer would chat to her of their fellowship in humanity. Such moments leveled the ground. These were griefs and annoyances that she, too, had experienced (though more time would have to pass before she would feel it possible to lead off with her own little troubles). Moreover, people do not talk of potato purée without there being a great deal else between them.

On this occasion, this one of so many, there may or may not have been some such irrelevant and yet so relevant dialogue between them before they set about what Mrs. Hill supposed she had to call "work." Sometimes the composer would appear fizzing with anxiety and eagerness to discuss some problem, and by discussion, Mrs. Hill felt, rather than as a result of anything she directly said, would come up with an answer. At other times he was more relaxed, though Mrs. Hill soon came to suspect that the outward calm and even affability screened a perturbation still more intense than when it was more manifest.

There is yet the chance that some documentary record of these sessions will eventually come to light. Scraps of paper might have survived, for it is more than possible that Mrs. Hill, rather than communicate through Thankful all the time (not that the girl was not charming and discreet) would have resorted to writing down questions and comments she wanted to address to the composer. He might have told her this had been his practice. That way she, particularly when points of musical grammar were at issue, even she not suspecting Thankful's facility, might feel secure that her meaning was being conveyed correctly. It is more than possible, too, that she would have wanted, when she left the composer some time in the early afternoon, to gather up such scribblings and take them with her to write up in some journal or memoir. This is all very plausible, just as it is plausible that Thankful, perhaps in her later years back on Martha's Vineyard, would have been visited by some scholar or biographer intent on interviewing someone who had been privy to the composer's intimate relationships and creative life, and who might have preserved some mementoes. Indeed, it is bewildering that A. W. Thayer, the first to plan a thoroughly researched life of the composer, and a man born and educated in the Boston area, should have taken himself to Europe to pursue his endeavors and not sought out this star witness living, so to speak, right under his nose. After all, Thankful, whose later existence is lost to us, could have outlived several generations of musicologists; she might even have survived into the twentieth century.

But to return to the day in question, Mrs. Hill immediately found – and Thankful has surely warned her as they walked through the house – a gentleman in some turmoil.

When she entered his field of view, and as if in answer to some question from her (though she had not yet spoken), he said: "But everything went wrong!"

"What do you mean, my very dear friend," said Mrs. Hill. "Whatever can you mean?"

The composer patted the chair beside him at his desk, and she sat down.

He looked at her squarely in silence for a moment, waved a hand at Thankful to go prepare the chocolate, and began.

"It was not I who chose Mr. B." – almost certainly, Mrs. Hill would immediately have suspected the composer was referring to Mr. Ballou – "to write the text." Yes, then, this certainly was to do with

Hosea Ballou. "I was assured that the Society had commissioned him to write it."

The composer slowly leaned forward toward Mrs. Hill in a way that might have been unsettling had she not been used to him by now, and his voice dropped as he went on: "I could foresee with the utmost assurance that to collaborate with him in this undertaking would certainly be difficult."

He leaned back again, and, while he was doing so, Mrs. Hill might well have been pondering whether she was being invited to defend Mr. Ballou and, if so, how she would go about doing so, when the composer continued, again in full voice.

"Now, however, several passages" – he picked up the little book and shook it – "indeed I may say a great many passages" – he put it down again and snarled the next words – "in B.'s oratorio" – he returned to a calmer demeanor – "will have to be altered."

The pause went on, and Mrs. Hill vigorously nodded, which suited as a prompt to the composer to return to his theme.

"I have in fact marked a few of them and shall soon finish marking the rest. For although the subject is very well thought out" (as, Mrs. Hill considered, I would expect of Mr. Ballou) "and the poetry has some merit" (not so sure) "yet it just cannot remain as it is at present."

The composer turned his head toward the

window. A bird was calling out, but of course that cannot have been what drew his attention.

Mrs. Hill felt she must now say something in support, and, forgetting for an instant that Thankful was not there to translate for her, she opened her mouth to do so. However, neither she nor anyone else could know how she was going to proceed, because at this the composer immediately directed himself once more to her and to what was on his mind.

"Well," he said, "we need not enquire into the *value* of poems of this kind."

Mrs. Hill again gave a firm nod.

"But so far as I am concerned, I prefer to set to music the works of poets like Homer, Klopstock, and Schiller."

Mrs. Hill would have been able to smile knowledgeably at the mention of these names, which she may even have revered as much as the composer did, and which now evoked memories of her German governess, memories that perhaps prompted her smile more than did mention of the celebrated authors. She had read what was the most celebrated work of Friedrich Gottlieb Klopstock (1724-1803), and almost certainly the one of which the composer would have been thinking, *Der Messias*, just as she had read Homer and Virgil in the original. Cousin Josiah, for all his praise of her, was not an unmitigated supporter of female education ("I do not speak of you, my dear, but of generalities"); five years before all this, as Mayor of Boston, he had been instrumental in closing the city's high school for girls.

Her smile beginning to drain from her lips, Mrs. Hill might have felt called upon to indicate her approval and her attention with a decisive nod.

"For at any rate," the composer went on, "even though in their works there are difficulties to overcome, these immortal poets are worth the trouble."

At this point, Thankful returned with the chocolate, so that Mrs. Hill now had greater opportunity to participate in the conversation. The composer sipped his chocolate, looked at Thankful with a smile, and turned to his friend to speak.

"What do you think?"

"Well," said Mrs. Hill, "I hardly have the experience or the authority to comment on those venerable authors, whose works I endorse as heartily as you do."

It was true, then. She did know Klopstock and Schiller.

"But if –"

The composer broke off her thought. It was as if what he was looking for was not her words, as transmitted by Thankful, but the sway of her mind, for which he needed no interpreter, seeing the evidence for himself.

"That is the reason for my asking you to help me," he said.

Mrs. Hill had, of course, been tremulously alert to where this conversation might be heading. Was something being required of her? If so, what? Or was she being ridiculous in supposing that the composer, however rapidly their friendship had developed in closeness, was about to invite her assistance in the great enterprise? But it did seem so. He had asked. He had asked, and he was looking at her in expectation of an answer – looking at her and not at Thankful.

She might answer, then, without words, but words came to her.

"Of course I would – I will – do everything in my power," she said, breaking off with the phrase still lifting, for it was clear by now that her response had been received. The composer had, almost at her first words, begun shifting things around on the desk before them, which caused Mrs. Hill to notice that he had open not only the manuscript booklet of Mr. Ballou's libretto but also two copies of the Bible, in English and in German.

Bringing the libretto to the fore, he pointed to a passage and said: "But how weak and poor are these words!"

Mrs. Hill read them, and then read them out – not for the composer's benefit, of course, but to experience how they felt and sounded:

O doth the wild ass bray when he hath grass?
Or doth the ox fed in its stall then beg?
Would we the cellar full of salt let pass
To give some savor to our white of egg?

She pushed the dismal booklet away from her and said: "Not one of Mr. Ballou's best inspirations, no."

"May I?" she added, and the composer gave her a quick nod. She reached for the English Bible and quickly found the relevant section, which she also read out:

Doth the wild ass bray when he hath grass?
or loweth the ox over his fodder?
Can that which is unsavoury be eaten without salt?
or is there any taste in the white of an egg?

"I think I see what has happened here," she said. "Your author" – to name Mr. Ballou would have seemed too much to blame him – "has found an almost regular line at the beginning of the first verse, and then has twisted and cramped the rest to complete the quatrain. With rhymes, of course."

The composer, looking at her fixedly all this while, said: "What can I do?"

Mrs. Hill did not directly respond, but instead asked: "May I see what Martin Luther made of this same passage?"

Again the composer nodded.

Mrs. Hill reached for the German Bible, turned the pages to Job 6, and once again read from the chapter out loud, for there was no need for her to fear making some error in pronunciation:

Das Wild schreit nicht, wenn es Gras hat; der Ochse blökt nicht, wenn er sein Futter hat.

Kann man auch essen was ungesalzen ist? Oder wer mag kosten das Weiße um den Dotter?

"How fine," said Mrs. Hill. "How very fine." And perhaps unconsciously she imitated the manner of approval her governess would voice during German lessons. "Simple and direct. That opening half-verse: four syllables and then another four. And the movement from statement (animal) to question (human), where the English has only the latter."

"However," Mrs. Hill continued in a different manner, "the problem with your libretto is that it has not sufficiently digested, if I could put it so, the Biblical text. We have to consider what Job is saying here, which is that God has given him the wrong food: the bitter aloes of correction, when what he has merited is the acceptable sustenance of the righteous – and this is the reason for his lament. The Biblical language is, we observe, full of metaphor, and I wonder if this is suitable in the libretto of an oratorio, where, of course, it is the music that will supply the poetry."

Mrs. Hill felt she had probably better stop there, for though the composer had given every sign of trust, she was uncertain how far and for how long she would be welcome on the sacred pastures of his work.

She need not have worried. Placing a palm on Ballou's booklet, the composer slid it back across the desktop in her direction, put his hands in his lap, and said: "You can do what you like with it."

Mrs. Hill thought. She picked up a pencil and opened the libretto to the aria they had been discussing. In the ample margin to the right of Ballou's text she wrote:

> *No creature cries before its proper food —*
> *Hold — the tasteless tests us.*

Now that she had written this down, she looked at the words, which seemed to have an extra sense, as not only a parallel or replacement for the text to their left but a commentary. Below, after a moment's further thought, she appended a version in German:

> *Keine Kreatur schreit vor seinem guten Futter —*
> *Halt — das Geschmacklose uns probiert.*

Then, with the same gesture of holding the book down on the desk with her palm, she moved it across to the composer.

Thankful, with no part to play in these exchanges, nevertheless observed closely what Mrs. Hill had written.

While the composer, too, was examining the lines, Mrs. Hill wondered if she should point out the alliteration, the rhythm.

Any such quandaries were rapidly dispelled by another of the composer's smiles as he pushed the little book back to her.

"I shall agree," he said, "to whatever you consider to be the best."

32 – From a Journal of July 1833

Sunday 21st [1] Mama [2] & Papa [3] came over to Quincy

---

[1]   Excerpted without alteration from the journal kept by Anna Cabot Lowell Quincy (1812-99), edited by Beverly Wilson Palmer as A Woman's Wit and Whimsy: The 1833 Diary of Anna Cabot Lowell Quincy (Boston: Northeastern University Press, 2003). It may seem curious that the summer pages of this journal fail to mention the presence at Quincy of the composer. However, Anna Quincy was writing for the eyes of two of her sisters who were traveling in the South – Abigail Phillips Quincy (1803-93) and Margaret ("Margy") Morton Quincy Greene (1806-82), the only one who had so far been married, in 1826 to the botanist Benjamin Daniel Greene (1793-1862), and "the only beautiful one" among the sisters, according to Charles Francis Adams (1807-86) in his diary entry for September 4, 1824 – and therefore would have confined herself largely to people they all knew. It may further be noted that the journal as a whole refers only very seldom to music, and not at all to any piano practice on the part of the diarist. This must cast doubt on the theory that the composer's so-called "Fifths" (Quinten) Sonata, No. 5, in A major, of his

before church.[4] Mama told me the new plan
of Susan[5] & Sophia[6] accompanying Papa to
Niagara[7] this week— All went to church— Mr
Brooks[8] preached— After church exchanged

Sechs leichte Sonaten, Op. 155, was written for Anna Quincy,
however attractive the notion of him punning on the young
woman's family name and, it has also been suggested, on
her position as fifth daughter. This Miss Quincy went on to
marry a Boston cleric, Robert Cassie Waterston. Surviving
all her siblings, she would have been the last to remember the
composer at Quincy, unless her nephew Josy – Josiah Phillips
Quincy (1829-1910) – retained some memory from his fourth
summer.

[2]   Eliza Susan Morton Quincy (1773-1850), daughter of a
prosperous New York importer of European goods.

[3]   Josiah Quincy III (1772-1864), whose long life took him
from colonial times to the era of the Civil War

[4]   The Quincys attended the First Church, where worship
was Unitarian. The building was relatively new, constructed in
1828 to replace a church of 1731 that the town had outgrown.

[5]   The author's eldest sister, Eliza Susan (1798-1882), who,
unmarried, served as her father's ghostwriter and wrote a
memoir of her mother.

[6]   The third daughter of the family, Maria Sophia (1805-
86), who also remained unmarried.

[7]   Josiah Quincy's purpose in visiting Niagara is unknown.

[8]   The Revd. Charles Brooks (1795-1872), remembered
for his work in educational reform in the state. A marble bust
of him, sculpted ten years after this occasion by Thomas
Crawford, is in the collection of the Los Angeles County
Museum of Art. His house at Medford, five miles north-west
of Boston, is on the National Register of Historic Places.

greetings with the Quincy world[9]— The Peturbed[10] rushed forward & armed me to the carriage. In the afternoon— all went save Mrs Miller. [11]— Mr Brooks as uninteresting as well could be[12]— Attention some what distracted by a form in Mr Whitneys[13] pew, which I at

---

[9]   That world would have included members of other families long established in the town, such as the Bracketts, Cranches, Greenleafs, Appletons, etc. Among the congregation on this Sunday, too, might well have been a former President of the United States, John Quincy Adams (1767-1848), and his wife Louisa, recorded in Frederick A. Whitney's booklet on the church (see below) as regular attendants.

[10]   Frederick Augustus Whitney (1812-80), who was three months younger than the author and a senior at Harvard. He took after his father, Peter Whitney, in becoming a clergyman, though following a period at First Church, Brighton (1844-58), he devoted himself to historical pursuits. Among his publications is An Historical Sketch of the Old Church, Quincy, Mass. (Albany: J. Munsell, 1864). He was forty when he married, his wife forty-three.

[11]   Mother-in-law of the eldest son of the family, Josiah Quincy IV (1802-82). She seems to have been looking after her grandsons Josy and Sam. Josiah Phillips Quincy and Samuel Miller Quincy (1832-87) both acceded to family tradition in entering the law. The elder brother was to follow his grandfather and his father in serving a term as mayor of Boston; the younger achieved the rank of colonel in the Civil War and was afterward advanced to brevet brigadier general.

[12]   The reader may to some extent judge, as the Revd. Brooks published several of his sermons.

[13]   Peter Whitney (1770-1843), a Quincy cleric.

first thought was Mr Hill[14], Miss Carolines[15] attendant[16], but who bore a strong likeness to Luther Angier[17]— After church, we encountered in the porch, & I found it was he— 'twas himself— but just as we were exchanging a few words— The Peturbed again rushed forth seised my hand & bore me away— Brought Mr and Mrs Cranch[18] down to the place— Had a very pleasant visit from them.— Mama returned[19] after tea.—

Monday 22d Excessively warm— Did nothing remarkable.—

Tuesday 23d Cooler—

---

[14]   Captain Charles Hill.

[15]   Caroline Whitney (1801-?), Peter Whitney's daughter.

[16]   In the sense of fiancé.

[17]   Probably the Luther Angier (1799-1881) who was to become the proprietor of an apothecary store in Medford.

[18]   The Cranches rivalled the Quincys in wealth and connections, and had a house in Quincy (which remembers them in its Cranch Street and Cranch School). Perhaps the Quincys' visitors this Sunday evening were William Cranch (1769-1855), a nephew of the nation's second President, cousin of its sixth, and from 1806 chief justice of the Circuit Court of the District of Columbia, together with his wife, the former Nancy Greenleaf. Their descendants included a son who published poetry (Christopher Pearse Cranch) and a great-grandson who made more of a name for himself in the same line (T. S. Eliot).

[19]   To one of the family's urban residences, in Boston and Cambridge.

33 – Yet Another Midday Meeting

fff "Are you satisfied?"

mf "My dear friend, my very dear friend, how do you think I could possibly be 'satisfied' when you are so evidently dissatisfied – indeed, if I may say so, disturbed? You must know there is nothing in this world I would not attempt in order to render you benefit, and how very far it is from my desires to do anything that would cause you grief or distress of mind."

ff "And why did you conceal your need from me?"

f "As I have said, I know no need other than to work for your good." *mp* "It is an honor beyond what I can say that you have taken me into your confidence with regard to this noble work on which you are embarked. These last days have seemed to me the very pinnacle of my life. In my elder years, here I am in a garden I was not prepared for, but have entered with relish and wonder."

⌒ *mf* "Is it really true?"

mf "Can you doubt my word?" *mp* "Absolute truthfulness, sir, has been the principal condition of my life." *mf poco cresc.* "Should I abandon it now? In my dealings with" *sfz* "you?"

⌒ ⌒ *p* "And whom am I to trust?"

p "It is not an appropriate question to ask of me, my very dear sir. You have had the opportunity to see in me, to find in me, what qualities I possess. It is for you to judge the nature of those qualities."

⌒ *pp* "I have not forgotten."

ppp "Thank you."

sffz "How did he get hold of it?"

f "Please!" *mp* "My very dear friend, there is no proof that anyone 'got hold,' as you put it, of anything. The fact that Mr. Brooks chose to preach yesterday evening on a text from the Book of Job is neither here nor there. It is the merest coincidence. The poor man has to find his subjects somewhere in the good book. And whatever Freddie Whitney —

subito ff "So he must have heard something about it." *subito mf minaccioso* "Of course I know the reason for his behavior."

ff "Freddie Whitney," *mp* "my dear, dear friend, is a young man whose mind skims like a dragonfly, just as his actions make it seem he is still trying to fit himself into his body. Please, please set all this aside and proceed with your great work. I will not demean myself so far as to protest that I have kept your secret as you asked me to."

⌢ *p* "Forgive me, but I am feeling exhausted."

mp "As I can well understand. I never saw so much paper fly across a desk, much of it destined for the basket below, which poor Thankful has had to empty every half an hour."

mf scherzando "She has a sweet tooth and that may account for a good deal.

mp "I am glad you reward her." ⌢ *f* "But be that as it may," *mf* "you are not to concern yourself any further with this ridiculous misunderstanding, which is entirely based, after all, on hearsay and on people who have absolutely no notion of your importance to the world of music. Let me go further: your importance to all humanity." *mp sotto voce* "Why else, you old oaf, do you think I have been spending all this time trying to assist you?"

mp "Forgive me if I hurt you. I myself suffered just as much."

mp "More, I have no doubt. And all for nothing at all." *mf enfatico* "Remember who you are! Remember what name you carry!"

p semplice "What a sad discovery you are making!!"

p espressivo "Sad? No, my dear friend. I have discovered that you have a thin skin. I have discovered that you will jump to the wrong conclusion and thereby cause yourself unnecessary suffering. I have discovered that you are susceptible to what you interpret as a slight from a poor innocent fool." *mp* "And how has it come about that I, Hannah Hill, widow, seventy years of age, have made these ⌒ discoveries?" *ppp* "Excuse me, but I cannot go on."

⌒ *mf* "I have acted wrongly, it is true–" ⌒ *mp* "Forgive me." *pp intimo* "Forgive me."

pp sempre intimo "There is nothing to forgive." *ppp morendo* "There is nothing, nothing to forgive."

p "I have no control over it."

pp "I know. I know, my dear friend." ⌒ *mp* "Come, it is time I left you to your work."

mp "Remember me and do so with pleasure – Forget my mad behavior."

p "Remember you?" *pp* "Yes, I will remember you."

mp "I forgot the chocolate today."

34 – A Monologue

"My life. My life. My life," she would have said,
Mrs. Hill would have said, Hannah Hill would have
said. "Let me tell you my life. Let me tell you my life.
Let me tell you my self. Let me give you my memory.

"I search for a place at which to start, and it comes
to me to begin with my husband, Dr. Hill. My Aaron.
My Aaron, a man of such calm and gentleness. The
strains, he would say, had all happened when he
was at sea, when he was serving as a naval surgeon,
for yes, he was a physician doctor, not a doctor of
theology. A man to make you well.

"That was not all he was, of course. As a boy, he
had joined the Continental Army. So I married a
soldier as well as a sailor. And I married a merchant,
which was another part of his life in Portsmouth,
where we were married, in 1785 – I was twenty-
one at the time, he a few years older – and where

we lived for several years, before he came into his father's estate in Cambridge, and we then moved thence. The estate was a large one, and its management required a good deal of his attention: buying seed and animals, replacing tools and machinery, supervising our laborers, finding the best markets for what we produced, trimming our trees, maintaining our accounts, and, of course, dealing with all the domestic servants we inherited with the house. Then, just when the whole thing was running in perfect order, and he felt he could install a manager, an admirable man, thoroughly trustworthy, my dear restless Aaron, at the age of fifty, took on a new responsibility as Postmaster of Boston. It was, of course, an honorary position, and, he would say, an honor. It was, though this he would not say, a gesture of respect from the city, not so much for his past services of various kinds as for his probity and his serene demeanor.

"But here I am, speaking of someone you never knew and never will know," she would have said, "and certainly never will nor can know by way of my paltry words. A widow speaks. Is there more to it than that? A poor widow, her husband of close on half a century not three years departed. Be kind to her. Treat her kindly.

"How can I give you his presence? How can I bring him into your mind, as I might usher him into a room?"

"Perhaps I could do so by my own presence, by being with you, sitting with you, as we have sat so much and so often these last weeks, being together, so much as to loosen the tightness with which we normally feel ourselves straitened into our own bodies, loosen it so much that we feel we float a little into the air. Being used to one another: perhaps this is what I am trying to say. Being so used to the soft roughness of that voice, to how that rounded body can spring from that chair, so used to these things that they are no more alien than the archipelago of spots on the back of your hand. What is alien is when they are missing, when they are no longer there, and you feel yourself no longer yourself, as if a part of your own body had gone, and could not be found, and could never be found.

"I do not know," she would have said, Hannah Hill would have said, "if you have ever had an experience such as I am failing to describe, ever had such knowledge of a person, ever held such presence of a person as I am trying now to have you hold.

"I know so little of you, my dear friend, so little of your past – only what the world knows, which is that you traveled to Vienna to study with Dr. Haydn, that you have lived in that city ever since, writing symphonies and sonatas and concertos and operas and quartets –.

"I stop," Mrs. Hill would say, she would say, "I stop. Why tell you this? I tell you what anyone could tell you. I cannot tell you what perhaps I alone at this moment could tell you – though I am sure there will have been others, we have lived so long – which is your present, your present and your presence, just as I cannot tell you of the present and the presence of my husband, my Aaron. He has gone now, and he has taken some of me with him – perhaps the part that could have explained, that could have told you of him.

"Perhaps it was the same part of me that would go, that would leave me," she would say, "when he would go from our house into the city, or only as far as the vegetable gardens at the far end of the estate, but then I would have it, still. I would be stretched out through so many hundreds of feet, through so many miles, as honey is stretched by a spoon from a jar. But now the thread is broken," she would say. "I am back in myself, all in myself.

"When there was a part of me abiding with him," Hannah would say, "abiding *in* him," Hannah would say, "I was so much more. I extended through space," Hannah would say. "The extent of me went through vacancy; I filled vacancy; vacancy held for me no fear," Hannah would say. "I knew roses and hydrangeas; in their season. I knew tulips and anemones. I was with them. I was in them. I knew streets and wagons, and women on corners selling lavender. I knew wind," Hannah would say, "and the clatter of hooves on slate cobbles. Sitting at home," Hannah would say, "reading in my parlor, I knew the scents of yeast and cinnamon from the city's bakeries. I knew," Hannah would say, "the splashings of the sea at the wharves and the calls of the gulls and a fellow yelling," Hannah would say, Hannah would say, "from high up a mast."

Hannah. Oh, Hannah!

"Now I am tightened within this little body of mine," she would say. "Not so little, I should say. The moon rises out of the evening mist, and it is not mine. Nothing of it is mine. More than this: I myself am not mine. I do not recognize myself. I do not feel myself to be myself. How I will respond to that person who has just asked me a question, how I will raise my arm, how I will reach my hands behind my neck to fasten a chain – things I have done since I was a girl, things I have been doing for sixty years and more – are now strange to me. I do them, but they are not mine.

"Even my children," she would say. "I look at them through unknown eyes.

"Let me tell you of my children," Mrs. Hill would have said. "Let me tell you of William and Hannah and Harriet and Anna and Susanna. Let me tell you of my sweet Sophia, who left us so long ago, and of young Tommy, who went even earlier, lost at sea, but who had given us, just before he took his last leave, our dear granddaughter Mary, whom you have met.

"But none of this will tell you of my self," Hannah

Hill would have said. "The more I say, the less I tell you of my self. I want to tell you of myself, but I find it is not to be done in words," she would have said. "It is not to be done by speaking; it is to be done by silence.

"When I speak," Mrs. Hill would have said, "when I speak to you, I hardly recognize my self. Whether in the one speaking or in the words spoken, I hardly recognize my self. I feel myself to be someone else, quite suddenly to have become someone else, the moment I opened my mouth, someone apart, who now speaks of her self, which is not my self. I feel absent, waiting, waiting for my lost self to return and fill me up, for my self to be poured into me, as milk is poured into a glass, or rather as if a glass might fill itself, with milk, with this white opaque liquid of my self, which, however, I can never see, and from which I can hear no words, because it has no words – not like whatever now speaks to you – because it exists before words. It exists in silence. It exists in the depths of me, where there is no sound, in the dark depths where there is no sound and no light. I speak, and it is gone. The glass stands empty. I fall silent and it comes, as now it will, when I cease from this."

35 – The Indian Operetta

If it seems very possible – if unprovable – that a lot of the work on the oratorio was accomplished during the weeks at Quincy, especially during the latter part of this summer vacation, doubt and confusion remain with regard to other projects on which the composer might have embarked at the time, and which in some cases he might even have fulfilled. The so-called "Quincy" Quartet, to which reference has already been made, is a case in point; so is another work mentioned earlier in these pages, the "Fifths" Sonata. As already indicated, there is no certain Quincy connection with regard to the latter work, the surviving materials for which – some sketchbook notations, an early version of the trio that might have been written out as an Albumblatt, and the fair copy submitted to the publisher – do not, it need hardly be said, use the so-called "AQ ink." There is no reason to suppose the work was not begun some months after the composer's return to Vienna, in late November 1833. Sadly, a document that might have helped clarify the chronology of this sonata and its companions – a request from Bernhard Schotts Söhne precisely for "six easy sonatas" (*sechs leichte Sonaten*) – disappeared from the grand ducal library of Wolfenbüttel before its date had been recorded. As for the quartet, attempts to identify it with the extraordinary work in A flat the composer published in 1835 as his Op. 162 are entirely speculative.

There is a little more substance, however (though caution is needed), to the thesis that the composer did at least start to venture at this time upon a work of which the trace he left in his correspondence has long tantalized scholars: "It is impossible for me to give an opinion, especially with regard to the Indian Operetta."

Some background here may be useful. It is known that the composer's host at Quincy, Josiah Quincy III, interested himself in the artifacts and the lore of the Wampanoag, who, at the time of his boyhood, still had some presence in the Quincy area. There is, indeed, some evidence that he knew at least a little of the Wampanoag language, which he might have learned from a family servant, a boyhood friend, or, perhaps less plausibly, from published sources. The question has therefore been raised whether this single record in the correspondence of an "Indian Operetta" might not relate to a libretto his host had prepared for him. Needless to say, nothing of any such libretto survives, nor is there any evidence that Josiah Quincy, or, indeed, any member of his family, took any interest in the composer's musical work while he was in residence with them, still less that any of them actively collaborated with him in the function of librettist. Mention has already been made of the composer's absence from the journal kept by Anna Quincy. Nor do we find his name appearing in the extensive correspondence maintained by Hannah Hill, a widowed cousin of Josiah's known to have been staying at Quincy through a large part of the summer of 1833 with her granddaughter Mary.

That was how the matter stood until quite recently: a solitary mention by the composer of an "Indian Operetta," unsupported by any further documentation of such a project, and that mention, as has long been recognized, ambiguous. The composer might be referring to a libretto that has been submitted to him or written for him, which he is unable to judge because he has no knowledge of its language (English, as it might be, or perhaps Wampanoag). Alternatively, he might be alluding to a work on which he is, at the time of writing, engaged, and which he cannot discuss, either because it would be contrary to professional decency, not to mention his own moral rectitude, for him to discourse on his own endeavors, or because the composition is still at an early stage. In their rush of hope for such an opus by the composer, whether fully achieved or only sketched in part, scholars have tended to overlook a third possibility, that the composer has in his hands an "Indian Operetta" by someone else, on which he is unwilling to comment because the score is manifestly incompetent, or perhaps because it is the work of a friend, acquaintance, or admirer of his.

However, this last interpretation, having been raised, may perhaps now be laid to rest. By collating two documents not previously considered together, we seem to find that the composer may indeed have made a start during his weeks at Quincy on an "Indian Operetta," though to a libretto that came not from within the Quincy household but from quite another source. One of these documents is a draft page that previously presented something of a puzzle. It is clearly a solo vocal line, untexted, with some suggestions as to accompaniment. Written out in what we may for the moment agree to be "AQ ink," it looks at first blush as if it might relate to some part of the oratorio. However, there is nothing in the latter work with which it in any way corresponds, and it has therefore customarily been dismissed as an *ébauche*.

The other document that suddenly gains relevance here is a page in the hand of Henry Wadsworth Longfellow, evidently detached from some longer work, for it carries the page number "16" and is torn down the whole length of one side. This page had universally been relegated by Longfellow scholars to the vast store of drafts the poet made in advance of his most celebrated work. However, the watermark on the sheet of paper in question indicates indisputably that it comes from stock made for Bowdoin College, where Longfellow was a student between 1822 and 1825, and professor of modern languages between 1829 and 1835, thus giving us a *terminus ad quem* for this draft almost two decades before he began work on *The Song of Hiawatha*. To the contrary hypothesis that the poet was here using a sheet, or several sheets, he had been holding in reserve all that time, we may be bold in our rebuttal, for this would have been completely out of accord with what is known of his working practices. Moreover, the penmanship is very definitely that of the young Longfellow, in his mid-twenties, not the mature and very well experienced writer he was to become. Dating the draft to before 1835, and therefore to before his second European tour, during which he encountered the *Kalevala*, has, it need scarcely be said, profound and even exciting implications for the genesis and, indeed, the originality of the

Hiawatha epos. What concerns us here, however, is this draft's relevance to creative opportunities that were available to the composer, in Boston and through the summer at Quincy.

Perhaps the strong trochaic rhythm of the afore-mentioned vocal draft should have been noted earlier. Placed alongside the Longfellow page, this draft reveals itself at once and unmistakably as a setting, breaking off after the ninth of the poet's thirty-one lines (on this page, we should emphasize, which clearly transmits only part of the work, or intended work). The passage that was, we may now say with confidence, set by the composer runs as follows:

> Tell me truly, Manabozho,
> By the cloud upon the mountain,
> Swear it by the salmon circling
> In the deepness of the water,
> Swear it by the panther prowling
> 'Neath the twinkling constellations,
> Swear it by the purple loosestrife
> At the banks of weary marshes,

While acknowledging that wide intervals are char-acteristic of the composer's fourth period from quite early on (the Op. 142 clarinet quintet affords a particularly interesting comparison with the draft under review), it is impossible not to understand the intensification and even exaggeration in this Longfellow setting as ironic in temper. This then raises the question of the irony's direction, whether the composer was, with great if on occasion heavy wit, confirming the poet's stance, which was to convey by the orotund locutions of this passage an awkward and ridiculous attempt at grandeur on the part of the character, or whether the composer is here robustly mocking what he diagnoses as bathos in the poet's style. Doubtless, this matter will be pursued in further discussion of the two fragments.

A proviso is in order at this point. The reader will surely have observed that, though we may have come near demonstrating that the composer set lines by Longfellow, there is no proof at all that these lines came from the libretto for an "Indian Operetta," or that Longfellow ever engaged himself on such a task. This single page contains more lines than would seem likely for a number in an opera, *a fortiori* an operetta, and the character declaiming, if character it be, is still in full flow at the end. Moreover, the presence of the name "Manabozho" suggests that here the poet is gaining a glimpse of his great masterpiece, for this was how he styled the hero of his epic before settling on the form the world knows. We may note, also, that the page does not contain any indication of who is speaking (or singing); nor does it offer any stage directions. We must hope more pages from this draft will come to light and clarify the matter of whether we are dealing here with a quite separate project of the composer's or indeed with a morsel of his much discussed "Indian Operetta."

There are other questions that have yet to be satisfactorily resolved – in particular, that of how a connection could have been formed between the poet and the composer. Here we must look to the figure of Josiah Quincy. It was in December 1834 that Quincy issued his celebrated invitation to the poet to join the faculty at Harvard, on condition Longfellow return to Europe on a second educative expedition – an invitation and a condition that were both accepted. We therefore can be quite certain Quincy was aware of the poet by then. What we could wish for is some evidence of this awareness stretching back a year and a half, so that Quincy could conceivably have brokered a working relationship between poet and composer, possibly even invited the poet to Quincy so that the two could meet. Studies of the Quincy archives, long suspended, have recently been resumed at full force in light of the new information. We look forward eagerly to an early advance in knowledge.

36 – Diminished Concerns

"He will be returning to town early next week."

"With the score?"

"I can tell you only what Quincy tells me."

"He says nothing of the score, of the work?"

"He says only that he is pleased a cousin of his has been able to assist the musician."

"I was not aware of a Quincy with any pretension to musical expertise."

"Lawyers to a man."

"It is a large family."

"But not one, I think, the muses would lightly kiss."

"Come, come, we must be grateful to them for allowing us to situate our great guest outside the city during the heat of the summer. Remember what he said: 'To stay in town during the summer is torture to me.'"

"But I hope he will have remembered this was not to be entirely a holiday."

"Let us not all at once and every time fear the worst. I believe I read in one of the German journals that he very often accomplishes his greatest work when staying out of Vienna for the summer, at Baden or some other resort. That was precisely why I set myself to finding some similar place of refuge and respite on this side of the world."

"And why I sounded out my old friend and ally Quincy."

"I think we all had our parts to play."

"And Quincy, too, I apprised of our hopes, that in the peace of his estate, removed not only from the city's heat but also from its noise, its incessant activity, its perpetual present, its now, so inimical to creative reflection, our composer would be able to complete his great work. An oratorio, I said. A compositional edifice that would resound –"

"Can an edifice resound?"

"– through history, and would carry the name of Quincy with it."

"Thus we, minor inhabitants of the hive, nurture the monarch in expectation of our great prize."

"Are we sure Mr. Colburn will be available at this notice?"

"So we do. And next week we shall have it."

"At any rate, next week we will know."

37 – A Farewell

It is Thankful waiting for her. Mrs. Hill has been called down, and it is Thankful waiting for her. It is Thankful standing in the entrance hall with a folded piece of paper in one hand. Mrs. Hill would like to talk to the girl, but is very well aware by now of Thankful's reluctance to emerge from an oceanic silence. She takes the paper with a smile and a nod, and waits until Thankful has been let out by the footman and the footman gone. Then she turns her eyes to the piece of paper in her hand. Then she raises it, opens it out, and reads.

"The night before last I had a dream in which you seemed to me to be in *a stable*, where you were absolutely bewitched and captivated by a couple of splendid horses, so that you forgot everything around you…. How much is there that I would fain say to you to-day; but I am too weak. I should like to thank you 9000 times for all your efforts on my behalf.

"To what shall I compare your loyalty to me, your affection for me? Indeed I am deeply in your debt for so much affection and for so many kindnesses you have shown me. I can never forget it. I only wish that I could return this kindness in some way. And why should I not do so?

"I would gladly have had another talk with you. I am fond of you. Is it any wonder? Continue to be my friend; you will always find me the same. Oh, I admit that I do not deserve your friendship. That too is the truth.

"Your approval is dearer to me than all else in the world. Please keep me in your memory. Don't forget me.

"There are certain emotions which it is impossible to describe.

"The weather is becoming colder. Have a pleasant journey – and think of me occasionally. But do not be anxious about anything. Everything will be all right.

"Well then – now I shall cease from chattering.

"One thing more. I must add that *everything around* and near us compels us to be *absolutely silent*.

"Farewell! … Farewell! Take care of yourself. God be with you. God be with you. God be with me and with you."

38 – An Announcement

"But now," said the composer back at Myrtle Street that evening, once his three guests, or more properly his host and his two guests, had come in to his room and, at his gesture, settled themselves on the two sofas, these three gentlemen whom he had called at so important a moment, for such they understood it to be, being the same three who had, it seemed so long ago, welcomed the composer to this distant shore from faraway Europe, which none of them had visited, or would visit, but which remained for them constantly the model, positive and negative, for what they were here perfecting, whether in a piano factory or in the composition of a hymn, or in the leadership of a great society dedicated to divine art, these three being Jonas Chickering, Lowell Mason, and Samuel Richardson, to list them in alphabetical order, whether by surname or by first name, it

makes no difference, among whom Mason had
taken his place on the smaller sofa, the one against
the wall facing the window, leaving his companions
Chickering and Richardson, both of whom, of
course, would have known the layout of the room
far less well, Richardson quite possibly never having
been there before, leaving them to share the larger
one and so confront, and be confronted by, the
composer, who, up to when he had begun to speak,
had maintained silence, offering no greeting but
only that gesture of the hand for them to sit, to
find themselves places, whether with deliberate
intent or not, the two guests having been led up the
stairs by Mason, who had then held the door for his
colleagues so that he was the last of the three to enter
the room, with Richardson going in first, befitting
his eminence within the Society, then of course
Chickering and so Mason, who, though last, was
ready, and there is no way of knowing whether his
action was prepared in advance, or spontaneously
decided, or completely unconscious, to seize the
advantage of the smaller sofa, on which he could,
without ostentation, sprawl a little diagonally and so
discourage either of the others from sitting beside
him, not so much because the proximity of either
of them would have been an annoyance, a nuisance,
or an inconvenience, as because this situation, on
the smaller sofa, singled him out and, what was
very likely more important in his mind, whether

consciously or unconsciously arrived at, gave him a commanding view of the three others present, four including Thankful, who sat on the piano stool, but facing away from the instrument, out to the room, with the composer in his armchair, as so often, not that Mason had it in mind, as far as anyone might tell, that he would, for some reason he might or might not guess at, require a position of dominance, since he was very sure, as were the others, that the composer had summoned this meeting in order to deliver himself of some pronouncement, which they had to suspect would be something of weight and moment concerning the great work they had commissioned from him, and which they had to hope would bring them joy and satisfaction at last, in which case there would be no need for much discussion but rather for celebration and congratulation, but the lack of a clear strategy on Mason's part, or of the need for some strategy, would not have kept him from grasping at what he might have perceived, again not necessarily consciously, as an advantageous tactic, this occupancy of a site within the room that enabled him to keep half an eye on his two confederates while quite naturally and innocently focusing his attention on the composer, because one never knew what these two, or any two, might have been planning, separately or together, to answer whatever it might be that the composer had called them here to disclose, for that surely

would have been his purpose, was his purpose, in
requesting this meeting, or some might rather say
demanding it, not that they were unwilling, any
of them, to come here and to be here, not in the
least, for they would surely have been hoping and
expecting that the composer, at the end of his long
sojourn at Quincy, would have something to impart
to them, and they would surely have been expecting
and hoping that this something would have to do
with the oratorio, for Mason had several times
assured the other two, Richardson and Chickering,
that the composer was fully aware, "apprised" was
the word he used, fully aware of his responsibilities
in this matter, to the Society, as an august but also
distinctly abstract entity, and to them personally,
who had invested so much trust in him that he would,
having undertaken to come here, having indeed
made the perilous voyage, and having spent all this
time in Boston and in Quincy, not now disappoint
them, for this was to them unthinkable, though
alas they did now and then have to think it, consider
it, even if for all of them, it may be said with a fair
degree of confidence, their hopes would indeed have
been higher, that the composer, that their composer,
as they were coming to think of him, yet mindful of
his universal and timeless rank, as they sat here, was
about to divulge at least some schedule of when he
would be able to deliver the score, when they could
complete the casting of the principal roles, when

they could begin rehearsals, and so forth, so that
the great work would now, as the composer spoke,
slide in time with his words, slide across noiselessly
from the sphere of the hypothetical to that of the
actual, and that they could relax into a smile, an
inward smile, in the knowledge that their oratorio,
which none of them could not but think of as their
oratorio, because of how long they had been delib-
erating upon it, hoping for it, looking forward to
it, if probably not imagining it in any sense, that
the moment would come when this great work, as
they also called it, because it would have to be such,
would take on its earth-shattering reality, at some
date they could fix and be sure of, and not remain
forever a chimera, so rapidly becoming an embarrassment, to its composer, or perhaps one should
say non-composer, and to them, but to them most
of all, to the three of them sitting there, as they had
feared, as they had been fearing, as they had come
together several times to fear together, but which
they need fear no longer, beginning from this point
in time, since here was the composer arriving at the
end of his silence, having judged his silence long
enough for dramatic emphasis, following the way he
had started the sentence, with all of them listening,
Thankful as well, waiting to hear how it would go,
though this she surely knew, how it would end, and
as it turned out it was more than they could have
hoped for, more than they indeed had hoped for,

much more, so that for an instant they were caught off guard, these three gentlemen of the Society, and for that brief instant could not tell whether the news was good or bad, the best or the worst, what they had eagerly hoped for or what they had gloomily feared, even anticipated, him concluding, "it is finished."

39 – And Immediately, a Visit

The two gentlemen had gone down the stairs, and his father with them. The coast was clear. Lowell Junior, who had reached the age of ten during the time the European gentleman had been staying with them, walked across the landing from the room he shared with his elder brother to the door through which his father and those two others had recently exited. He held up his fist to knock, stopped himself for a moment of second thoughts, and knocked. It was, of course, Thankful who came to the door. From observing her, he had picked up a little of her sign language, and, without his thinking about it, this was the means by which he made his wish known to her.

"Please, may I come in and see the gentleman?" he signed.

"I'll go and see," she replied, in the same manner, and closed the door.

Half a minute later, she opened it again and silently beckoned him in. Though he could see, behind her, the gentleman in an armchair looking searchingly in his direction, in he firmly went.

That, however, was the limit of his bravado. Thankful closed the door behind him and assumed her position close to the composer, while Lowell stayed where he was, just a few feet into the room.

Having deemed the silence to have gone on long enough, realizing that the boy, to have come in here at all, must have come with some purpose, and understanding the difficulty the boy might now have in expressing that purpose, the composer decided it was up to him to break the ice.

"Well," he said, "I don't know what to suggest."

Though no more than ten and a quarter, Lowell junior had a fair knowledge of German, in which his father had begun instructing both him and Danny around the time Billy was born. He therefore responded to the implicit question briskly in the language in which it had been uttered.

"*Bitte, mein Herr, würden Sie gerne Dame spielen?*"

Thankful, of course, could not deal with this. Since it was her invariable practice not to risk hurt or embarrassment to the great man by speaking in his presence, she indicated to Lowell in sign language that he would have to frame his replies in English. He signaled "sorry" and began again.

"Please, sir, would you like a game of checkers?"

Quite suddenly and unexpectedly, the European gentleman laughed.

"I will gladly play," he said, "– very gladly," and added: "At the moment I feel equal to anything."

At this, the boy, similarly electrified, rushed back to his and Danny's room to fetch the board and the box of men. When he returned, the European gentleman got up from his armchair and indicated they should set up the game at the table by the window, where they could sit opposite each other, with Thankful between them at the third chair, looking out into the dusk.

Thus it was arranged, and play began, at first in silence.

Quite some years had passed – more than half a century, indeed – since the composer had last played *Dame*, and his technique was rusty. Not so young Lowell's. He would play whenever he could persuade Danny to join him, usually on the promise of some reciprocal favor, and so it was almost inevitable he should soon take the advantage.

"Impossible!" said the gentleman, as Lowell, with one of his black men, leapt over two white, his opponent having fallen into the most elementary trap, which Lowell had not even designed as a trap, thinking it so obvious, but only intended as a step toward a deeper ploy.

Having not quite succeeded in concealing a grin, the boy turned dead serious to answer the gentleman:

"No, sir, that's the way you take men," and he placed his two captives decisively back in the box.

They were not alone for long, and soon the gentleman was becoming almost jubilant in his defeat.

"He must go," he repeated in song, after each of Lowell's triumphs, to a three-note motif the boy would remember and much later recognize at a string quartet concert. There followed from the gentleman another cascade of melodic variations and repetitions on "Away with him!" All of these, however, slid quickly out of Lowell's memory.

At one point, the gentleman leaned back from the table, as if a longer perspective would offer a more optimistic view of the state of play. It did not.

"What a plight I am in!" he said.

"You haven't lost yet," said the boy, but the gentleman was not to be so easily consoled.

"No, no," he said, "it is too bad."

And then, with barely a pause, he leaned forward.

"You have such a splendid gift for music," he said, "why don't you cultivate it seriously?" – to which he added: "La musica merita d'esser studiata."

Lowell Junior and Thankful looked at one another nonplussed, and the boy thought it would be a good idea, not only for that reason, to change the subject to one on which he felt he and the gentleman would be more in accord.

"I don't suppose you enjoyed this evening's dinner very much...," he said.

The gentleman looked at him gravely before offering a comment.

"Today," he said, "there was no soup, no beef, not even an egg." But then his look altered in an instant as he exclaimed in high excitement: *"Te Deum laudamus!"* – a phrase the boy did comprehend, even as he comprehended how his anxiety about the modesty of the meal had distracted him from the game and opened an opportunity the gentleman had so gleefully seized.

"Oh, well done, sir," said the boy, as the gentleman, with a sharp clunk, dropped the first black man in the box to join the several white.

"I thank you," he said.

The boy stared at the board.

"Papa says," he said, "it does us good occasionally to imitate the early Christians and observe a fast, because our God is a wrathful God." He moved one of his men forward.

"You don't believe that, do you?" said the gentleman.

The boy looked up from the board to this friendly antagonist.

"No," he said. "I believe the Good Lord gave us the fruits of the earth for our benefit and enjoyment."

The gentleman smiled and made a counter-move, at which the boy spoke in a whisper.

"There's some cheese in the larder," he said. "I could go and get us some."

"That is indeed my most ardent desire," said the gentleman, with a comical pomposity the boy could enjoy, already standing up from his chair, but to be stayed when the gentleman spoke again: "I advise you to be as careful as possible."

"It's all right," whispered the boy. "My parents are in the parlor reading." And he turned to tiptoe out.

"So be careful," the gentleman called after him, also in a whisper.

There was not much time then for contemplating the board before the boy returned bearing a large plate loaded with a great hunk of cheese, half a loaf, and a knife.

"May God reward you for this, noble sympathizer," said the gentleman, as the boy placed his prize on the table.

Knowing that her hands would not be otherwise needed for a while, Thankful took charge of cutting the bread and cheese into manageable pieces, which all three of them were occupied in consuming before play and talk could resume. Then, brushing some crumbs from his front, the gentleman again examined the board. The last capture had been his, but how could it possibly be repeated?

"My situation at the moment," he said, "is very difficult."

40 – Preparations Commence

There would have to have been, a few days after this, some meeting again of the three gentlemen with the great composer they had – as it had turned out, so happily – invited.

In the meantime, now that the work of composition was finished, other work could begin. A messenger from Charles Bradlee of 164 Washington Street arrived the morning after the evening checkers match and cheese feast to place the loose sheets of the completed score in a satchel and carry the same to the company's offices, where parts were copied and the composer's manuscript bound in fine green leather, for this had been Richardson's express instruction, to form a conducting score. Even so quickly, as the messenger strode the sidewalks of Boston, the oratorio was being carried on again, from the realm of the imagination toward that of performance, of real sounding existence, where it would continue to exert itself down through the generations, never to return.

Even quite complex tasks are accomplished swiftly in a society of multifarious specialists that is still in its energetic youth, and inside a few days the bound score and the manuscript parts for the orchestra, the choir, and the soloists have, by the same messenger or another, been brought to Myrtle Street, ready for the already mentioned meeting of the Society members and the composer.

This time they are downstairs, in the dining room, whose table, cleared for the occasion, provides space for the musical materials to be laid out, the full score at one end, occupying the position of head of the table, and the various parts proceeding around it anticlockwise: strings, woodwinds, brass, timpani and percussion, choir, soloists. The four men, the composer accompanied always by Thankful, are circumambulating the table, on occasion picking up a part or taking it to one of the eight dining chairs that have been moved to the edge of the room. One or more of the four may have a notebook, and a Dunbar-and-Thoreau pencil, to jot down notes, and one or more of them at any given time may be doing this.

Silence is to be imagined, but eventually there will have to be discussion, no doubt in the same room, with the musical materials to hand, everyone now sitting. For Thankful, it has long become second nature to place herself where she can be seen by the composer, while the others distributed themselves as they would.

Who will be first to speak? The composer coughs. It will be him.

"It is a fine specimen of the wretched copyists I have had since Schlemmer's death," he says, alluding to the man who was his regular copyist, Wenzel Schlemmer (1760-1823).

"Herr Schlemmer was" – this is Chickering, the only one to spot the reference – "a paragon, his work revered in the musical world, though of course no specimen" – he emphasizes this word he is re-using, perhaps in an effort to revalidate it – "of it has ever passed before my eyes. Yet I know that Mr. Bradlee employs –"

The composer cuts him off, holding up, and shaking, the page he has in his hand: "Where there is a dot above the note a dash must not be put instead" – he returns the hand and the page to his lap, and his voice falls – "and vice versa."

"Quite so. That is indeed a notable error," says Richardson, who is not at all sure how he would interpret the mentioned notations differently, whether singing or playing his cello, "and must be corrected."

The composer, now shaking his head, is probably not paying attention. He gets up – Thankful

watches him with care – and returns to the table
to replace the miscreant page, and, as he does so,
starts at the discovery of something else amiss.
He shuffles through the sheets in one of the piles,
and says: "*Four horn parts* are missing. I have just
noticed this."

Mason rushes to join him at the table, goes
around to check if the absent parts have been placed
elsewhere, horns among the voices or violas. But
they are simply not there.

"This is most disturbing," he says, "most
disturbing."

"No doubt," says the composer, still at the
table, around which Mason is scurrying, "haste is
responsible for this."

Haste. Yes. Hasten on, you. Come to the end of
the meeting, when the participants have turned
from this tedious question of the accuracy of the
copying to the choice of soloists, now that the parts
for these, with whatever faults, may be inspected.

"We have parts, then, for six soloists," says
Mason. "Thank you in that, sir," – he is looking at
the composer – "for your moderation."

A stiffening in the composer's features is noticed
only by Thankful.

"The casting of the Divine Being," Mason goes
on, "I feel we should leave for a little reflection – we
all know the possible candidates – and therefore
so must we that of the three comforters: Eliphaz

the Temanite, Bildad the Shuhite, and Zophar the Naamathite." He relishes these names and takes a pause, to allow them to reverberate. As he does so, still standing, he looks from one to the other of his two colleagues before him in their seats. "The role of Elihu, whom the Bible distinguishes, as I recall, as the son of Barachel the Buzite, is to be taken by Daniel Gregory Mason. That of the principal actor in our drama was always to belong to our estimable President." He smiles in the direction of Richardson, who nods rather to acknowledge Chickering's applause.

Taking the nod as a request for silence, as perhaps it was, Chickering ceases clapping, and Richardson takes the opportunity to speak, addressing Thankful:

"Please say that I am very sensible of the honor the great composer does me, and that I will do my utmost to justify his trust. I would like to hope also for some advice from him."

Thankful passes on the message, and the composer replies:

"But your noble heart, which I know so well, certainly needs no injunctions."

Chickering then raises a hand toward Mason, who blinks and smiles expectantly.

Richardson, slapping his knee, bursts out: "You need not ask permission to speak, man!".

Chickering, emboldened, makes his point.

"You have not specifically mentioned," he says, "Mr. Colburn."

"Indeed?" says Mason. It is not a question. He leans down to pick up a piece of paper from the table, as if needing to consult it before answering, which he then does: "Marcus Colburn will sing the Devil."

"Excellent!" says Chickering, and then: "I wonder if I could take the part with me for a day or two. I would like to give it some study."

"Of course," says Mason, widening his arms.

"It is not for you to permit him," says Richardson as he rises, at which Chickering also gets up from his chair and holds out his hand to Mason, who, after making some play of not being able to find the part in question, gives it to Chickering with another of his smiles.

The meeting is over. Thankful goes to fetch the gentlemen's coats.

41 – The Job Ahead

The meeting has been called for twelve noon, and they are again assembled in the dining room at Myrtle Street, with the bound score and the parts on the table laid out exactly as before, but with this difference: that the parts have been emended. Charles Bradlee himself is there, to receive any further corrections, which he does not hope for, or compliments, which he discreetly but confidently does – compliments that would be coming from such a source, for he can hardly believe, though he has the evidence of his own eyes, that this tidily dressed man sharing the same room, the same air, is the musical lion of the age and not some illusion. Thankful, of course, is close by. Also present are, again, Richardson and Mason. Chickering is last to arrive, and be shown in by Bobby.

"I hope I have not delayed anything?" he says.

"No, no," says Mason, and the clock on the mantelpiece releases its twelve neat chimes.

Chickering probably suspects that none of the others – not Richardson, not Mason, and surely not the composer – will have remembered he took the part for the Devil with him, and he is probably right. That being the case, he will have to wait for an opportunity to deliver the little speech he has prepared.

Mason, who has been counting the bell strokes, is ready to resume speaking while the twelfth is still echoing.

"Gentlemen," he says, "we have two principal items on our agenda: the status of the parts, which Mr. Bradlee's excellent staff – and most especially his chief copyist, Mr. Rampel – have been inspecting and correcting most assiduously these past days," – smiles are exchanged between the two men – "and the final details of the disposition of the solo roles. Might I suggest we begin with the former, so that we may allow Mr. Bradlee to return with dispatch to his offices, where I am very sure his absence is being regretted even as we speak?" More smiles. "Our distinguished guest – and, if he will allow me, my friend – has been examining the parts since they were brought back here on Monday, and I should now let him unfold his findings."

Thankful has not thought it necessary to transmit all of this to the composer; there has long been an agreement between them that she should omit anything superfluous or unnecessary said in his presence, and, in order not to be seen with her hands still, simply keep signing phrases such as: "He does go on so," or "More of the same." But now, of course, she tells the composer he has been invited to speak again on the condition of the parts.

The composer stands.

"Obbligatissimo –" – he nods to Bradlee, who smiling returns the gesture – "but the marks 'piano,' 'crescendo,' 'diminuendo,' etcetera, etcetera, have been horribly neglected and frequently, very frequently, inserted in the wrong place. For God's sake please impress on Rampel to copy everything exactly as it stands. If you will just have a look now at what I have corrected, you will find everything that you have to tell him. I can't understand why your people have not strictly adhered to my score. Why, I have spent no less than the whole of this morning and the whole of the afternoon of the day before yesterday correcting these two movements" – he pages through the full score to indicate the two of which he speaks – "and I am quite hoarse from cursing and stamping my feet."

Bradlee, from silent amazement and gratification at being in the presence of the composer, feels the blood now filling his cheeks. However, he will try to stay calm.

"Is it not possible, my dear sir," he says, "that

some of these mistakes – dare I suggest all? – may be traced to your original manuscript?"

From watching Thankful, the composer turns to stare at Bradlee. Still holding the man with his eyes, he pulls a notebook out from his pocket, and reads:

"Page 5, bar 22: instead of e–a–f–d there should be e–a–f–e. Page 8, bar 9: instead of F there should be D."

He holds the notebook up in Bradlee's direction and riffles through its pages, nearly all of which are covered with writing. He then thrusts the notebook toward Bradlee, who cannot but take it.

No longer feeling so assured, the publisher is determined to stand his ground, nevertheless.

"Nevertheless," he says, "I know from long experience how composers, in the heat of inspiration, are not destined always to be accurate in notating their intentions."

From the composer comes a snort.

"As for mistakes," he says, "I scarcely ever required to have them pointed out to me, having had from my childhood such a quick perception, that I exercised it unconscious that it ought to be so, or in fact could be otherwise."

This would be the moment for Bradlee to yield, and the three Society members look down at their feet when it becomes clear he is not minded to.

"Sir," he says, "even the greatest masters make mistakes."

"Mistakes!" the composer yells, "Mistakes! You yourself are a unique mistake!"

There is a pause. No-one moves until Bradlee again speaks.

"Gentlemen, you will excuse me. I left important business at my offices in order to be with you here. I will send a boy to collect the materials again and bring them back to us for correction – with, of course, any further schedule of errata from the composer."

He stuffs the notebook in his pocket and leaves.

Mason rises from where he has been sitting to again take the floor.

"May I suggest," he says, "we add the name of Mrs. Cuddy to those of Miss Belcher and Mrs. Long to complete our trio of ladies?"

Richardson leans forward and says, with a glance toward the gentleman in question: "What is the composer's feeling?"

"I should like," replies the composer, turning to Richardson, "to have *your* opinion about this."

"Then," says Richardson, "I would propose Mrs. Washburn."

"Mrs. Cuddy," says Mason, "has the larger voice."

"Mrs. Washburn," says Richardson, "the sweeter – and, I would add, the more accurate."

"Chickering," says Mason, "what is your view?"

The piano manufacturer, however, has not been following the conversation but only waiting for a gap into which to insert his memorized statement. Now, suddenly, here it is. He stands up.

"The composition is majestic, and, I would say, fearful. It breathes fire. It soars, and will soar into the hearts and minds of those who hear it. It has the superb luster of Lucifer and the demonic egoism of the Prince of Darkness. In it Mr. Colburn will be magnificent," he says.

He places the part back with the others on the table, his hand reluctant to come away.

42 – A Gift

It would most likely have been early in September
– not at the end of the month, as originally planned
– that the composer returned from Quincy with the
Lowell Mason family, the change made because, at
some point in the summer, the performance date
was brought forward to October 27th. We must
now be in mid-September – perhaps this is the 20th,
when the package is resting on that table, unopened
– during the lull between the conversations that
followed the score's completion and the beginning
of rehearsals. But though the composer's task is now
done where the oratorio is concerned, by no means
is he idle. He will have other compositions on which
he is working – music that, at this present moment,
is in various stages of advance: in the midst of being
written out in fair copy, still needing some polishing,
as yet disordered but with a clear end in view,
approximately drafted in part or in whole, roughly
sketched out, existing only in inchoate thought.
Who would risk displacing his attention, at whatever
level it may be focused? Earlier this morning, when

the mailman knocked at the door and Bobby went to answer, he might have been working on the alternative scherzo for the "Quincy" Quartet or on one of the Six Easy Sonatas. Right now, as he goes downstairs to see if there is some lunch, he might be leaving behind on his worktable a draft of one of the songs that will form the cycle *Psalms of the Land*, to words in English by a poet who preferred to remain anonymous.

Abigail Mason makes sure there is something available at this time, even if he has expressed a wish to go for a walk and find something – an allowance from the Society is distributed to him as he needs – at the Exchange Coffee House on Congress Square or one of the taverns on Washington Street. But no, that will not be necessary on this occasion, because here is Abigail appearing in the hallway and indicating – she has not had sufficient opportunity to learn Thankful's sign language, but has an effective command of mime – that some potato soup is available, with perhaps some bread and a glass of Meldrum's beer. The composer nods his thanks and goes into the dining room to be served – in solitude, because no-one wants to disrupt any thought processes that might be going on even when he is away from his desk. In any event, Lowell is at the bank, the two older boys at school, and the younger two with Abigail in the kitchen. When he is seated, before Abigail has brought his lunch, Bobby takes in the package – a box about three inches by five inches by seven inches – and puts it down on the table beside him. For the moment, he will only look at it, look at the thick cream paper in which it is wrapped, the scarlet sealing wax, the handwriting. Abigail comes in with the soup, the bread, the beer, all on a tray, from which carefully and silently she places these things before him, together with a spoon.

"I thank you heartily for this attention."

Perhaps he has learned to say this in English.

Food has to come first. He tears off a piece of bread after consuming each mouthful of soup, and occasionally sips at the beer. All the time he is looking at this little parcel. He must know who sent it.

He finishes his meal, takes the package in his hands, and slowly tears away the paper. It is as if we could hear the breaking of each fiber. Inside is a silver-gray box with a silver-gray lid. Let him not delay. He opens the box and eases aside the tissue paper, also silver-gray, folded around the contents. He sees a card of the same color, with writing on it in spare lines of black ink. The writing is upside-down to him. Good. He will leave it till later. As he lifts the card, before he can see what lies beneath it, he has the sensation of fine cloth at his fingertips. Then he can see it. What is it? His first thought is that he has been sent a table napkin, a plain white table napkin. But as he feels it again, he is aware of multitudinous gentle corrugations. He pulls it out. Yes, all white, it is covered with symmetrical patterns of tiny squares and stars supporting larger elements, nested dodecagons. He extends it between thumbs and forefingers, and holds it up to the window, whose light brings out, in soft yellow-gray shadow, the intricately embroidered and so subtly defined design picked out in white silk on the white cotton. Releasing one of the corners, he touches the thing again with his free hand, the right. The embroidery is not only a wonder to the eye, its myriad fine ridges enhance its delicately sumptuous, almost voluptuous feel.

He picks up the card. Of course he recognizes the hand. He turns the card over, and finds the sender has provided a German translation. He turns the card back again.

> The Pin is not the Pencil –
> The Needle cannot speak –
> Nor note of sorry Music
> Will any Stitch evoke –
>
> And yet I ask you – Listen –
> However it appear –
> Within this white of Silence
> A Song is written there –

43 – The First Rehearsal

God is here
Near
And divine
Mind
Speaks

Most of the Society's many singing members, and perhaps all the women joining them, will have been practicing already, alone at home or else in small groups, but this is the first full rehearsal with the orchestra, which is also drawn from the membership, for the Society is most essentially a band of enthusiastic participants. It is also at this point limited to men, and the women volunteering for the chorus will probably be the wives and daughters of those same men, but zeal for music – or zeal for the very particular genre of oratorio, where music can join hands with religious education and moral uplift – brings together a fair social mix. Among those admitted to the Society most recently are a shoemaker (Eben F. Gay), a chair painter (Silas Allen, Jr.), two cabinetmakers (Daniel and Volney Wilder), and a bookbinder (David C. Long), as well as a "professor of music" (James Hooton). The Mastersingers of Nuremberg might feel themselves at home – though the Society has yet to welcome a member from among those listed at the back of Stimpson's Directory as "Persons of Color."

Here they are, on the raised stage, a great wave of faces producing such noise. Harmonies robust and colossal are being sounded – or, as it might seem, sounding themselves, through these assembled people – for the first time, thrilling and exciting those who utter them, and in uttering hear them. It is one thing to sing a single line, with your hands on the piano keyboard striving for impossible stretches, or to put together a few parts with friends of an evening, but now to be here, to be one among many, part of a conglomeration of voices and instruments – to be contributing to and caught up in a great mass, slowly swinging like a giant bell, or moving forward inexorably in a slow charge – is an experience they can in no way have anticipated. You are in the music, and the music is in you. All else goes.

"Ladies and gentlemen, could we try that again?" Lowell Mason, of course, is conducting.

God is here
Near
And divine
Mind
Speaks

Nobody in the choir has arrived here more
thoroughly prepared than Jonas Chickering, who
knows his part, Tenor I, by heart – though he
holds his copy of the choral score in his hands
like everyone else, for it would be a horror to him
to make an exhibition of himself – and who has
marveled already at the harmonies summoned
from one of his own instruments by the eight parts
making their stately yet wayward progress. His
wife and sons, so often roused from their reading
by a *sforzato* from the music room next door, know
the work as well as he does, he who has come here
with the music, he would say, in his voice. Now,
however, with his voice enmeshed with those of
others, he feels it to have been taken from him. He
is used to singing in chorus, and therefore to being
aware of his own voice as an interior echo. So it is
now. Its sound is familiar. What is strange to him,
and without precedent, is its separateness. He feels
that what he hears, as a hum within his skull, is not
being produced by him but rather installed within
him, that he is not singing but being sung.

"Much better, but could I hear more from the

second basses? You are the buttresses of this great
church."

> God is here
> Near
> And divine
> Mind
> Speaks

The rehearsal is taking place in the Society's
regular venue, Boylston Hall, the top (third) floor
of Boylston Market, built twenty-three years ago at
the west-side corner where Boylston Street meets
Washington Street, a block from the Common, to
a design of typical elegant plainness by Charles
Bulfinch, whose brick-Classical style, if no longer
quite in fashion, was such a success around the turn
of the century, bringing him commissions not only
for the Massachusetts State House but also for that
of Connecticut. Called to Washington for a decade
and more, Bulfinch is now back in Boston, and,
assuming that at seventy he could still climb the
stairs, he might be attending the rehearsal, hearing
what his hall sounds like with this great work within
it, but more likely he is waiting for the performance,
a month or so later. The hall is a perfect double
square, a hundred feet by fifty, similar in size to
Zankel Hall, the performing space that was to
be constructed below Carnegie Hall almost two

hundred years later. Zankel would be able to hold an audience of almost six hundred. Concertgoers of 1833 might be used to more cramped conditions, and so perhaps Boylston can accommodate a thousand, particularly if, as we may presume, it has a balcony.

"Now I think we are beginning to get the measure of it. Shall we try it one more time?"

> God is here
> Near
> And divine
> Mind
> Speaks

On that balcony, probably chatting in whispers just now, are the three female soloists: Miss Belcher, Mrs. Washburn, and Mrs. Long. Their first names are lost to us as surely as the color of their eyes, or how they wear their hair, or what attire they have put on for this semi-formal, semi-public event at ten in the morning. All we know of them, besides their last names, is their voice types: soprano, mezzo-soprano, and contralto, respectively. Perhaps Mrs. Long is the wife of the bookbinder who joined the Society last year, but she could equally be married to Edward J. Long, clerk, a member of three years' standing. Details of women singers will not be published for another generation.

"Excellent. We are now filling out the power of this music, but we risk doing so at the expense of words. Articulate, please! Once again...."

> God is here
> Near
> And divine
> Mind
> Speaks

"Thank you. Now if we could just find again that force we touched before. Last time, ladies and gentlemen."

> God is here
> Near
> And divine
> Mind
> Speaks

44 – Enter Satan

Mr. Colburn waits outside the back doors of the hall until he hears the chorus ending. He has not been listening to the music, only listening for it to finish. Any peculiarity in the cadence, therefore, has passed him by. He opens the doors and strides down the central aisle, removing his wide-brimmed fawn felt hat with a sweep of his arm, while taking care not to dislodge the gold-blond wig that rests somewhat oddly on his florid complexion, and thus, aiming for grand politeness mixed with insouciance, he greets the assembled company.

"I do hope," he calls out, with the voice of a practiced actor, "I do not arrive at this momentous occasion *en retard*."

Not until after he has delivered his line does he recognize that what he has in view is not Lowell Mason's back but the front of the man, his arms and his long white baton raised to the balcony, where Miss Belcher, Mrs. Washburn, and Mrs. Long are by now standing, their parts open before them, and alongside them three of the orchestral musicians: a trumpeter, a clarinetist, and a bassoonist, all having just taken their instruments from their mouths. It will have been the second number they were beginning, a quasi-fugue initiated by the said wind-instrument trio, emerging from the close of the choral introduction without a break, to be taken up eventually by the three female soloists.

Should Mason utter any word of reprimand? Probably not.

Chickering is smiling.

"You were about to come in," says Mason.

"My dear," says Colburn, "but I *have* come in."

Chickering's smile is threatening to turn into a laugh.

"Quite so," says Mason, before quickly changing to a fresh tone. "Why do you not come up here, by us?"

"Should I not be down here, in Hell?" says Colburn. "I believe I am to sing the Devil."

Mason does not respond, does not move, but waits while Colburn places his hat on a seat at the front of the orchestra, and takes off his dark-green greatcoat, his scarf in a lighter, brighter shade of green, and his fawn lamb's-leather gloves, finger by finger.

Having an eye on this divesture, which proceeds with all the ceremony of a nuptial mass he attended once at Holy Cross, Mason is reminded also of a conversation he recently overheard between the composer and young Lowell (in whom the great artist, so generously and so hearteningly, is taking a notable interest) – a conversation on the topic of, among all things, clothing. Or perhaps his mind turns to that conversation in order to distract itself from the display Colburn is offering to his captive audience, numbering – what? – surely a hundred and more. Bookbinder Long joined as No. 359 in the roll of members, but, of course, some will have died or left over the eighteen years since the Society's foundation. Perhaps the active membership now is around two hundred, and perhaps half of those are committed to this performance. To them must be added the ladies of the chorus and probably also some instrumentalists who regularly take part in the Society's performances but remain outside its ranks. An example from the earlier years would be Louis Ostinelli, who was the normal concertmaster though not a member. It is therefore impossible to know how many are present this morning. Mason is considering, rather, a conversation he overheard last night between the composer and Lowell Junior, and in particular this word of advice from the composer:

"…similarly the best material for the trousers too – By the way, do not wear your good clothes indoors. Whoever may call, one need not be fully dressed at home…"

"Perhaps there is in this banal matter of apparel," Mason muses, "a kind of philosophy." He is, needless to add, ignorant of Thomas Carlyle.

But Mr. Colburn has readied himself by now, and come up the few stairs on to the stage, where he stands to one side of Mason, with Sam Richardson and young Danny further along. With one hand he smooths down the skirt of his burgundy redingote, worn over pants in a bold check of light and dark olive-green.

"I think it will do us all good," says Mason, "to start again from the commencement of the fugue. Ready up there? Give us the B flat major chord you sustain from out of that orchestral clamor. But this time, I wonder if we could have it pianissimo, as marked, and not mezzo-forte?"

The trumpeter, clarinetist, and bassoonist will now have to take their instruments to their lips again and blow. They produce a second-inversion chord, from which the bassoon and afterward the trumpet fall away, to leave the clarinet holding the keynote for half a slow triple-time measure before it announces the theme, definite and at the same time mysterious. Nobody present, none of the hundred or so, has heard anything like this. Even Mason, who has been studying the score for a week, and playing it through at the standard model Chickering in his drawing room, is unprepared for the effect of the lone clarinet sounding in empty space. He nevertheless maintains his strict beat, for none of these musicians can be relied upon to feel the metrical flow. The others enter with the theme, bassoon followed by trumpet, and when the interplay has proceeded so far that another entry is due, the mezzo-soprano joins the clarinet, and with her a high haze of violins and piccolos. She also brings to the theme words, beginning with a curve of several notes to enfold in a warm embrace the name of the protagonist:

> Job – my Servant, my Son –
> I see into your Soul –
> And can you visit mine?

As for how the orchestra sounds, some clue is provided by a report from just five and a half years later, published in the April 13, 1839, issue of the recently founded Boston paper *The Musical Magazine*, and covering Handel and Haydn Society performances of Neukomm's still evergreen *David*, given on seven consecutive Sundays. One problem was imbalance in the orchestra, which had "eleven stringed instruments to fourteen wind instruments, of which latter seven are brass, – a most outrageous disproportion." Another "great and general fault" was the lack of ensemble, for "every singer and instrumental performer goes through his part as well as he can, without any other connection with

the others, and with the whole, than that of time...
every one is too ready, not to say earnest, to make
his particular part as conspicuous as possible; and
many times seems too willing to accomplish this,
sometimes by playing louder than the rest, and
sometimes by putting in extra notes and graces or
shakes."

For particularities of Mr. Colburn's art, we have
the testimony of Henry C. Watson, writing in the
March 18, 1842, number of the New York weekly
The New World. Colburn's voice, we read, is "of
good compass and sweet in quality...combining
strong contrasts of *piano* and *forte*." O.K. so far.
Then, however, comes something about "intensely
laboring lachrymose pathos." And it goes downhill
from there: "...no execution beyond hackneyed
cadences in the slowest possible time, and these...in
the worst possible taste."

Here he is now as Satan, not so much interrupt-
ing the fugue, perhaps, as twisting it, as a fallen tree
trunk will twist the flow of water in a stream.

> What if –
> What if –
> What if you Changed?

The composer is there, hearing nothing, feeling
every note.

45 – A Protest

The back doors of Boylston Hall burst open. A man enters, and for a moment he stands.

It is the Reverend Ballou, who has come huffing and puffing up the stairs to the hall, where at his precipitate ingress the surging music frays. This is not the first rehearsal, at which Danny Mason was already showing such a penetrating yet delicate command of Elihu's great solo, and there will have been several more sessions, taking place on weekday evenings, enough for word of the oratorio to have got around.

There is only one person in the hall whose attention does not immediately turn to this stout figure now proceeding up the central aisle with far more physical gravity and mental purpose than Mr. Colburn was minded to exhibit at his first entrance, and it is to that unnoticing person, seated on the aisle in the third or fourth row and now at last turning in his seat to see what everyone else is looking at, that the Reverend Ballou directs himself. He stops, just behind the composer and Thankful, both of whom stay sitting, not wishing to render any courtesy to this impudent arrival. Lowell Mason motions the chorus and soloists to sit down, while himself remaining on his feet and turning to observe. The Reverend Ballou, having stopped, takes hold of the lapels of his black frock-coat, one in each hand and begins:

"The nature or essence of God is infinite. It is evident there can be but *one* being in the universe possessed of an infinite essence, as infinite space itself could not furnish room for another." He pauses to inhale deeply and take in the space in which he finds himself. Not being much of a concertgoer, he has not been here before.

Thankful just has time to sign to the composer: "It is not as we thought." Right before they left Quincy, there was a brief discussion between them – in sign language, in which the composer has made a considerable advance – on how the Reverend Ballou would respond to the alteration, or, rather, wholesale rewriting of his dramatic poem.

Seeing a communication passing from the girl to the notable musician, the Reverend Ballou takes this to be a transmission of his opening remarks and continues:

"This true and living God is but ONE person. Now attend to the words of Christ, then judge whether he was that *person*. Alluding to the time of the impending destruction of Jerusalem, the Saviour has these remarkable words: Of that DAY and that HOUR knoweth no *man*, no not the *angels* which are in heaven, neither the *son*, but the FATHER *only*. Matthew 24, verse 36, Mark 13, verse 32. Undeniable inference: There is but one PERSON who is the only wise and all-knowing God."

He pauses, and makes a gesture with his hand for Thankful to convey this to the composer. The conversation that then passes between these two in signs is, however, more commentary than translation:

"It is theology, sir. Unitarian."

"What is one to do?"

"Wait. There will be more, no doubt."

While signing this, Thankful turns to the Reverend Ballou and speaks out loud to him: "The phrase 'neither the son,' sir, is in Mark but not in Matthew."

Not a whit discommoded, the Reverend Ballou goes on, as do Thankful and the composer, the former replying to the Reverend Ballou vocally while conversing in signs with the composer, who responds to her similarly. The composer, therefore, does not speak. If the Reverend Ballou thinks this strange, he does not betray as much. Perhaps he concludes that increased facility with sign language makes it possible for the composer to express his meaning in full to Thankful, who can then speak for him in English. That would certainly ease exchanges for interlocutors who lack the German of Tübingen.

Thus the double dialogue proceeds:

THE REVEREND BALLOU (*addressing* THE COMPOSER): I shall now show the manner in which the Apostles preached Christ.

THE COMPOSER (*signing to* THANKFUL): What is to be done?

THANKFUL (*signing to* THE COMPOSER): Have no fear. This is something I know about.

THE REVEREND BALLOU (*addressing* THE COMPOSER): Paul was said to have preached Christ in the synagogues, that he was the CHRIST, the SON of God: Acts 9, verse 20.

THANKFUL (*addressing* THE REVEREND BALLOU): In the beginning was the Word, and the Word was with God, and the Word was God: John 1, verse 1.

THE REVEREND BALLOU (*turning to* THANKFUL *and speaking more loudly*): We have seen and do testify that the Father *sent* the Son to be the Saviour of the world: First Epistle of John 4, verse 14.

THANKFUL (*addressing* THE REVEREND BALLOU *without raising her voice*): Who, being in the form of God, thought it not robbery to be equal with God: Paul's Epistle to the Philippians 2, verse 6.

THE REVEREND BALLOU (*addressing* THANKFUL *in a crescendo of scornful satisfaction*): In these specimens of Apostolic teaching we discover no Trinity in Unity, nor Unity in Trinity, nor God-man, nor Hypostatical Union, nor any other of those hard, unnatural, unscriptural and cramping names with which the Christian world has been perplexed for several centuries!

THE COMPOSER (*signing to* THANKFUL): The man is ill.

THANKFUL (*addressing* THE REVEREND BALLOU, *still evenly, and at the same time signing the gist to* THE COMPOSER): Christ must be the *omnipotent* JEHOVAH, because he said I and my Father are one: John 10, verse 30. And again, there are three that bear record in heaven, the Father, the Word, and the Holy Ghost, and these three are one: First Epistle of John 5, verse 7.

THE COMPOSER (*signing to* THANKFUL): I thought perhaps that the third person you mentioned was the former *King of Holland*.

THANKFUL (*signing to* THE COMPOSER): Now then....

THE REVEREND BALLOU (*addressing* THANKFUL *with total certainty in himself*): In answer to this, I observe concerning the three witnesses in heaven, that notwithstanding it is said they are *one*, yet it is not said *what one* they are! It is not said that these three witnesses in heaven are one GOD!

THANKFUL (*signing to* THE COMPOSER): I believe I now understand what is going on here. The Reverend Ballou is objecting to your use of three singers for the voice of the Divinity.

THE REVEREND BALLOU (*turning back to* THE COMPOSER, *concluding his argument*): I think the subject is by this time perfectly plain. You already perceive from the numerous passages quoted that the modern trinitarian hypothesis is wholly erroneous! May we all be willing to exchange our errors for the truth, for the truth alone has power to make us free!

THANKFUL (*addressing* THE REVEREND BALLOU *lightly and at the same time again signing to* THE COMPOSER): You will, sir, excuse me. Matthew 28, verse 19: Go ye therefore, and teach all nations, baptizing them in the name of the Father, and of the Son, and of the Holy Ghost.

The Reverend Ballou reddens as the composer rises, followed in that by Thankful, looks directly at his erstwhile librettist, and at last speaks:

"I will not suffer my composition to be altered by any one whatever, be he who he may."

The Reverend Ballou swivels on his feet and leaves, as noisily as he came.

46 – Sam and Danny

If it could be said that the part of the oratorio's protagonist is made up of a sequence of plateaux going through the work, these being defined principally by differences in level, which is to say in vocal register, with Job's blessing of God, early in the piece, making the bass soloist almost a high baritone, after which the singer must reach to the very bottom of his range for the opening of the magnificent lament, whose three subsequent verses then rise again, in alternation with the three comforters, their parts taken by the three female soloists, whom the composer cannot keep from thinking of as the Three Ladies, with reference to *The Magic Flute*, and for whom he initially planned a short section headed "Entrance" – an andante in C minor followed by two variations – to give them time to come down from the balcony to the stage,

so that by now, at the close of the lament-dialogue
involving the comforters, having reached again the
high territory of his first number, the solo bass can
then descend again in the second part of the work,
where the feeling is so remarkably different, before
settling into his middle register for his final contribution, which seems to resolve the work some way
before its ending, the voice now comporting itself
with composed affirmation, then Sam Richardson
is fully in command of his part, right from the
earliest rehearsals.

Though the composer gently protested that his
affliction ruled out any attempt at coaching, Sam
has been finding opportunities here and there to
put questions to him through Thankful concerning
matters of phrasing, accentuation, and vocal color.
Even so, and useful as anything confided by the
composer may have been, Sam's powerful interpretation has come principally from within – from
the nature and character of his voice and of the
mind motivating it. Several contemporaries much
later wrote down their impressions of Samuel
Richardson – more than in the case of any other
singer appearing with the Society during this epoch.
His was "a bass voice of marvellous ponderosity."
He was remembered "as a man of large frame, noisy,
jovial, jolly, generous, obtrusive, free and easy, not
too refined." He was "a tall, bulky, and muscular
man, of jovial aspect, with a radiant countenance

and powerful lungs. Added to this, one of his eyes was in true position, while the other sensibly verged toward a squint. I honestly think that a better Goliath could hardly have been found either in or out of the Society's ranks."

So it must have been with the role of Job. If these testimonies suggest a Falstaffian figure, such a one might equally play Lear – though unfortunately we have no reports of Richardson's Job to vindicate such a supposition. All we can do is strive to imagine, across such a distance of silence, his splendid voice, his oratory, and his huge presence in, say, the opening of the four-part lament:

> Let that Day cease to exist
> That saw me born –
> May Time now wrinkle and crease
> And seal it down –

What would have been more admirable in his interpretation of this passage? The continuity of line or the precise intonation within a narrow range at the very bottom of the bass staff and below? The stalwartness or the fragility? Or would it have been the accurate judgment of the Boylston Hall acoustics, which allowed Sam to make the room resonate with the boom of his voice or shrink in order to communicate his intensest, most inward pianissimos?

Danny is not having such a good time on this occasion, which might perhaps be that of the Friday evening rehearsal at the end of the first week of preparations, called as usual for two hours beginning at six p.m. By no means does he owe his place on the stage entirely to nepotism. He has a fine, clear voice that is true in pitch; no fruity wobble from him. Often he is engaged to sing an anthem – "Let the Bright Seraphim" or some such – at one of the churches his father regularly serves as organist, and gets sent away with praise and a dime. And though the composer has never before written anything specifically for boy soprano voice, one would hardly expect Elihu's aria to be other than expertly obliging and gratifying to perform, if also keenly challenging. Danny will, we may be sure, have enjoyed learning it, taking it into his voice, feeling his way and listening to himself with care around the sharp corners of awkward intervals and jumpy rhythms, doing all this until the piece has become for him a natural way of uttering:

> Green goes my call as I sing from
> tomorrow –
> You think a youth should do no more
> than play?

If the words "green" and "call" are on the same note, and on the same beat of the measure, they could be vastly differentiated in color. Young Danny is a practiced artist. He makes the aria sound not only fresh and spontaneous – green, indeed – but also an inevitable outcome of the words, as if there could be no other way to express them than in these melodic bounds.

Everything is startling and right, startlingly right, as it will have been at earlier rehearsals, until he arrives at the third line of the song, with its high A, for which he unwittingly substitutes the A an octave down, where his tone becomes suddenly coarse and breathy. He notices the error immediately himself, of course, and his voice fizzles out, causing the orchestra, which has been moving confidently with him, also to trail away.

Lowell Mason takes only a second to decide not to ask for this again and risk Daniel Gregory faltering a second time and so becoming nervous and embarrassed, making the juncture a trap that will be waiting for him on the next occasion.

"Thank you, ladies and gentlemen," he says. "Very good, everyone." He snaps his score shut and picks it up in his left hand. "Until tomorrow."

47 – Astonishment

It is another rehearsal. And it is another interruption, a light knock at the back doors that would scarcely be noticed were not Lowell Mason and his forces paused, poised between movements, which allows the possibility that the knock was again made by someone waiting for just such a break in the music, and was not really an interruption at all so much as a notification of arrival. Reasoning thus, and thereby extricating himself from the travails of Job, in which he has been absorbed for an hour, Lowell Mason remembers that people were due to come at this time, at three p.m. on this Sunday afternoon.

"Our visitors are here," he says to his musicians, then takes the steps down from the stage and walks swiftly to the rear to pull open the doors. George Edmands, one of the Society's trustees, is there, with their two guests, as arranged. The woman wears a long dress of supple, well-beaten beige leather over darker pants. The man has a coat of beaver fur, which he opened on entering to disclose a black linen shirt and pants like the woman's, supported by a belt stitched with red, black, and white glass beads in geometric patterns. The woman's only ornament is a necklace of rough pieces of coral. She also puffs intermittently on a long clay pipe, the sight of which, more than any smoke or odor from it reaching him, is enough to elicit from Mason a gentlemanly cough. The two guests are difficult to age, but clearly the woman is much older than the man, perhaps eighty to his twenty-five, though she has had no trouble climbing the stairs up here. She is also clearly the dominant figure, the man, though considerably taller as well as so much younger, standing a little back from her – in her shadow, it would be, if this were out of doors.

"Professor Mason," says Edmands, as if making a pronouncement for all time, "may I introduce Mrs. Wonkŭssis and Mr. Pohkintippŏhkod?" Mason keeps his bow to the dimensions of a nod. The woman's response, in a surprising bass register, might be a grunt or a curt guffaw.

There follows a short conversation in Massachusett between Edmands and Wonkŭssis. The young man does not speak. He never speaks.

"Mrs. Wonkŭssis," says Edmands, "wonders at so many people in one place. She asks if they are all needed to make the music."

"Oh indeed," says Mason, "and I would wish there were more of us."

Edmands translates this, and Wonkŭssis snaps a comment, which Edmands interprets:

"It must be big music."

"It is very big music," says Mason, "by the greatest composer in the world," and he signals to where the composer and Thankful are sitting, their heads turned this way, for Thankful will have indicated to the composer that there is something to be seen at the back of the hall.

Edmands tries to convey to Wonkŭssis the function of this personage, but is limited by his elementary grasp of Massachusett grammar and his no more than rudimentary vocabulary, so that the dialogue proceeds something like this:

EDMANDS: That man writing on paper sound. These men paper see make sing and spell artifact.

WONKŬSSIS: How could it be possible for the art of colored air to be written on fine sheets of paper? I would like to see such writing.

EDMANDS: We signs have.

WONKŬSSIS: And all these pale women and pale men are able to read your signs and in accordance with them color the air? It would interest me very much to inspect such signs closely and see if they would speak to me.

EDMANDS: That is so.

WONKŬSSIS: But colored air comes as the breath of one who will sing or another who will play on an artifact. Can anyone breathe another's breath? How is breath to be represented in signs?

EDMANDS: Our music different. We are kift.

WONKŬSSIS: In what way or ways different? I have heard pale women and pale men singing; they sing like us; they color the air like us.

EDMANDS: Very true.

WONKŬSSIS: But are your colored-air-signs, so to speak, holy? You do not answer when I ask to see them.

EDMANDS: Not always but here yes.

WONKŬSSIS: I understand. In this place the colored air you make is holy. This is one of your sacred precincts. It is no doubt forbidden that we strangers enter any further. (*She turns as if to leave, at which her companion does the same.*)

EDMANDS: No. Please. Honored person must hear.

By this time, Mason will have quietly withdrawn from a conversation he could not understand and returned to the stage to shuffle through his score and give corrections to his chorus and orchestra. Edmands extends an arm to invite Wonkŭssis to go on up the central aisle, which she immediately does, Pohkintippŏhkod a few steps behind her. Passing the composer, she shoots him a quick glance, her face unreadable, and takes a place on the front row. Pohkintippŏhkod finds a seat diagonally behind her. All this is done in silence, except for the skims of leather soles on floorboards. Hearing these, Mason looks behind him, waits until the visitors are seated, and turns back to his musicians. He would like very much to begin again from Danny's aria, but the boy is obviously under strain, and, in any event, the occasion would seem to call for something more spectacular.

"Gentlemen," he says, "No. 17."

The orchestral players find the place in their parts, and the movement begins. Though a single timpanist with two weak double basses will not, no question, be making as much colored air as the composer is evidently asking for here, the expression of divine presence cannot but come across as powerful in such a space. Mason looks back quickly at Wonkŭssis, who is staring ahead, impassive, unfocussed.

He looks back at her again just after he has brought in the full brass section *fortissimo*. Still nothing. The pipe is in her mouth, gently smoldering.

The three women soloists are up in the balcony, as they will have been from the beginning of this second part of the work. They now continue the fugue that was broken off before, the trumpet, clarinet, and bassoon with them. Wonkŭssis does not look up and behind her but stays with her eyes fixed ahead, expressionless.

When the fugue has rolled to its grand ending, engaging the full chorus for an apotheosis that discloses an unexpected form of the theme, Mason turns again to look at Wonkŭssis. Her posture and her features are unchanged.

Over the contrastingly subdued introduction to the next movement, however, Mason hears a curious muttering, excited but low in register as in volume. He turns his head once more, to see Wonkŭssis in mid-rise, her eyes wide and directed to the single instrument in use at this point: the organ. Muttering in the same way still, she walks toward the stairs and so comes up on to the stage. Pohkintippŏhkod, who got up as soon as she did, has sidled out from his row to go with her, some steps behind as usual. String players, woodwinds, and brass make way for them as they head for the engine in the center at the back, whose player, with his back to the hall and hearing only the music, is unaware of what is going on. Mason, who has been ticking time even though this is not necessary, lays down his baton, watches the visitors go, and moves to join them at the organ. With three people standing behind him, Charles Zeuner is at last aware of some disturbance and stops playing, so that Wonkŭssis's susurrating voice now stands out in the echoing space, repeating: "Penoowinneunkqusspinneat, penoowinneunkqusspinneat,...."

Had Edmands not stayed at the back of the hall, he might be able to translate what Wonkŭssis, in acknowledgment of the silence around her, goes on to say, staring at Zeuner: "What calls of animals of the evergreen forests where the sun never reaches and what roarings of the ceaseless winds from the heavy ocean do you make, o master, and what is the name of your heart-amazing artifact? See: the air is still thrilled with the orange and purple of its holy voice! Tell me, tell me, its name. Let its name be Mighty Horse. Let its name be Rainbow of Stars. Let its name be Silver Waterfall."

Though Zeuner could not, of course, offer such a translation, he understands the strength of feeling his playing has aroused. He waits for the lady to finish and nod to him, which he takes, rightly, as an invitation to play on. His hands set out on an improvisation, seemingly of their own accord, the left in the far bass, the right appearing to roll over and over itself up and down the keyboard, so that the organpipes disgorge a melody that goes from lusty to fluting and back again in endless variation of a phrase none of them can quite recognize. Wonkŭssis clacks her teeth as a sign of high approval.

It could go on forever: Zeuner occasionally turning his head to beam at the three behind him while his hands work at the keyboard, Wonkŭssis adding dental percussion, her young ally swaying his head, Mason taking mental note of ideas he could bring into his own playing. It could go on forever.

48 – An Interview

The boy is just two and a half months past his fourteenth birthday, but he has been an employee of the bank's in New York for more than a year, and has won the confidence and respect of his superiors – sufficient for them to accept his volunteering, even eager volunteering, to take a package of bonds, letters of credit, and other important documents to an associated establishment in Boston. He will not be able to stay long enough to attend the performance, of which he has read in the New York papers, but at least he should be able to get himself in to a rehearsal and see the great man. Best of all would be to take his friend Walt with him, but the two of them cannot come near affording a second ticket on the packet boat.

Having therefore made the journey alone – his first by sea – he finds lodgings for himself and discharges his duty at the bank, where he is told to return on Monday morning, this being a Friday, for a similar package to be taken back in his messenger bag to New York. His business done for the day, he can now go to Boylston Market and inquire about the hour of the evening rehearsal. Six. Hungry by this point, having walked all over the town, he goes into a chophouse, which not only fills him up but also neatly occupies the time till six.

There are boys of roughly his age in the chorus, and so he is able to enter the hall unquestioned. The other boys are all congregating in an area at the back of the stage, and so he goes there too. Since Professor Mason has been strict about not talking in the hall, this gang he has joined stands in silence. He notices that all the boys but him have leaflets in their hands. Peering at that held by the boy to his right, he tries to make out what is printed on these leaflets. What brought him here was the composer's name; he has no technical knowledge of music. Catching his stare, the boy on his right stares back, but then notices that this newcomer has not yet been given the music, and so offers to share. The new boy makes a brisk shake of his hand, palm down, and the other shrugs.

The conductor is on the stage now, at the front, talking to another boy, who has his eyes down at the floor. They all wait. Then the conductor dismisses the boy he has been talking to, picks up a sort of ivory stick, and delivers an instruction. The music begins, and the young bank clerk, squinting to his right, does his best to open and close his mouth when the others do. This activity keeps him from noticing until later that the composer, whom he recognizes from an engraving, has entered the hall with Thankful, and the two of them have taken their usual seats near the front.

There is a break, and he quickly goes down, before anyone else can, to the composer and this companion, or whatever she is, no-one else with them. Having approached, he stops still. They look up at him. He opens his mouth, but hardly has he done so when this soft-spoken but authoritative girl tells him he must address to her anything he wants to say to the composer, and she will translate for him.

"Ich weiß Deutsch sprechen," he says.

"Please do as I say," she answers, and so he does. However, he has not planned what should happen now, and the words that come out take him by surprise.

"I was wondering," he says, "if I might speak with the great composer."

Thankful has a choice here. She could transmit this boy's request, or she could deal with the matter herself. The boy, standing there, has a look of frankness and capability. The composer is no longer paying attention.

"There is a rehearsal tomorrow morning at ten," she says. "Come then, and I will see if you can speak to the composer immediately afterward."

"Thank you, miss," says the boy, hardly believing what he has been granted. He rushes out of the hall and down the stairs.

The next morning he goes to the hall in good time for the rehearsal. Again, he can slip in without drawing attention to himself. He sits at the back of the auditorium, and, when the rehearsal begins, finds his mind, with no anxiety now about being up on stage, plunging and rearing with the music. This is it. This is the sound of the great composer, so much more than what overwhelmed him at school when he went along with a friend to a practice session and read the name on the music stands. When it is over, he goes up to where the composer and his assistant are sitting. Seeing him arrived, the girl makes some hand gestures to the composer, who looks at the boy – it is a look he will not forget – and says: "But the discussion would have to last a short half hour."

The boy said he understood German, and we must assume this is so, however interrupted his schooling may have been. Thankful tells him he must reply in English to her, and she will translate what he says for the composer, beginning with: "Of course, sir. Thank you."

Thankful and the boy arrange three chairs in an

equilateral triangle, the boy gets out the notebook and pencil he always has with him in his bag, and the conversation proceeds, as thus written up by the boy from his notes:

A HALF-HOUR WITH THE WORLD'S GREATEST COMPOSER!

Q.: I must right away thank you, sir, for your gift of magnanimity and generosity in allowing me this most extraordinary opportunity to converse with you, and I decidedly hope you will not find the experience over-tedious.

A.: Accept my thanks beforehand.

Q.: Sir, you have come all the way from Europe to Boston to oversee the performance of a new oratorio of your own composition. Is there anything you would care to tell us, sir, about this monumental work?

A.: There is scarcely one part of it which quite satisfics me now. We are told that the best proof of sincere contrition is to acknowledge our faults; and this is what I wish to do. However, it will do as it is.

Q.: It is, if I may say so, sir, a work of incomparable power, but perhaps one whose complexity will not please the multitude.

A. Even if only a few people understand me, I shall be satisfied.

Q.: Yet, sir, what cannot fail to send thunder bolts through any listener is how the words, though very fine in themselves, seen on paper, are so much invigorated and enlivened by the music coursing through them like an ocean swell. I am reminded of something said by one of our great authors, sir: "It was not the same in the song."

A.: That is how things are.

Q.: I wonder if you perhaps, sir, coming as a visitor, find some difference of spirit in this land of free people –

A.: Freedom! What more does one want?

Q.: – whereas in Europe, sir, you must crawl to some king or emperor.

A.: *I shall never crawl* – My world is the universe.

Q.: Yes, indeed, sir. I had no desire to imply otherwise; and yet your position as an artist, as a discoverer on behalf of the many, is in no wise the same here, sir, in a society ruled not by a monarch but by our sedate councils of men elected for their wisdom.

A.: Well, that pertains to the science of politics, about which your friend knows very little.

Q.: Does art, then, sir, lie outside the domain of the political?

A.: Things are getting beyond me with this one.

Q.: Returning to your magnificent oratorio, sir, listening just now to this morning's rehearsal, I seemed to see before my eyes the very figure of Job standing against a landscape of barren gray-yellow earth.

A.: The description of a picture belongs to painting. On the other hand my sphere extends further into other regions and our empire cannot be so easily reached.

Q.: It may be, sir, the image came to me from the nature of the great sufferer's voice.

A.: If necessary, the bass voice could be altered to a tenor.

Q.: Really? I must say you astound me, sir. But if music is not, then, about pictures, what is its subject?

A.: It is about time.

Q.: Could I ask you now about contemporary practitioners of your art, the art you so dominate? What do you make of Kalkbrenner?

A.: It is now some time since I heard him. As it is, I am not very much in favour of mere virtuosity.

Q. Then the book of études recently published by Frédéric Chopin?

A.: It is a sound piece of work.

Q.: Mendelssohn?

A.: He shows great talent.

Q.: And what of the Fantastic Symphony of Monsieur Berlioz?

A.: Everything I built up has been blown down by a hurricane, as it were.

Q.: I understand, sir, you became very close to the late lamented Franz Schubert in his final months.

A.: The loss of my brother affected both my spirits and my works.

Q.: Could you tell me something of what you are working on now? I have heard talk of an Indian operetta.

A.: Well, there is not very much to say about that as yet.

Q.: *(If I had employed my better judgment, it may very well be that I would not have broached this topic, but I include the question here for the sake of the composer's response, which startled me by its force, as by its unexpected metaphor.)* How did you react to the controversial article adverting to your music that appeared recently in one of the German musical periodicals?

A.: I have not read the article. I no longer receive the paper, which is a shabby proceeding. If the editor does not rectify the statement, I shall cause him and his consumptive chief to be *harpooned* in the northern waters among the whales!

Q.: I believe I have now trespassed enough on

> your time, sir. Thank you. To meet you,
> to speak to you here, sir, has been a kind
> of dream.
> A.: Well then – now I shall cease from chattering.
> You can couch some things in better terms.
> Q.: By no means, sir. I shall record exactly what
> you have said.
> A.: God be with you.
> Q.: And with you, sir.

Back in his room, the boy wrote out several copies of his script, and on the Monday morning, before he was due at the bank, he took them around the offices of the *Boston Daily Advertiser*, the *Boston Journal*, the *Boston Post*, and the *Boston Transcript*. At three of these he was told to go away. The apprentice at the *Transcript* desk accepted his piece and gave him a half dime for it, but he could tell this was just out of kindness.

When he got back to New York, Walt, who had contacts with several newspapers, tried the article around for him but had no success. Had it been printed at the time, whether in Boston or New York, it would have given Herman Melville his first publication.

49 – The Breakfast Table (Again)

"Father, there is something I must tell you."

"You have my attention, Daniel Gregory."

"I cannot –. Sir, I cannot sing the solo."

"Daniel Gregory, I am surprised at you. Where we find difficulties, there precisely is the point at which we must persevere. Yes, you have had a slight head cold, but we are fast curing that with this honeyed tea."

"Father, I cannot do it."

"Lowell, my dear, Daniel Gregory is telling you. He is a boy. In little more than six months, he will be fourteen years old."

"I see. You know about this, Abigail? He has spoken to you?"

"I know about this, my dear, and so, so do you."

"You are right."

"And *you* are right, in that you knew but did not want to know."

"However, the performance is in three days' time. We cannot simply cut the number; it is central to the whole musical drama."

"You will not have to cut anything, my dear. The boys have made arrangements."

"The boys?"

"Yes, father. I have been teaching the part to Lowell Junior. He's very good. Better than I could have been. Better than I was."

"Lowell Junior?"

"Yes, papa. I can sing it now. I know every word."

"Ah, my boy, but do you know every note?"

"That too."

"Sing me, then, if you will, the opening phrase of the song."

"Green goes my call as I sing from tomorrow."

"Very creditable."

"My dear, why can you not say 'perfect'? The boy is perfect. Your son is perfect."

"As I say, very creditable. And the credit is due to you both – for, Daniel Gregory, you are clearly an excellent teacher. Of course, we shall have to inquire of the composer."

"We shall have, my dear, to *inform* the composer."

"Indeed. Thankful, would you kindly inform the composer that Daniel Gregory is indisposed, and that his place will be taken by Lowell Junior?"

Thankful gains the composer's attention and signs the message to him. He puts down his knife and fork before speaking.

"I was, indeed, not a little surprised when I found the boy in a distant room practising all alone, and neither disturbing nor being disturbed by others."

"Then I think we may take it that the composer, as in so many things, was there before us."

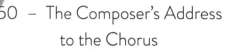

50 – The Composer's Address
to the Chorus

All hail to this rabble!

I am so very fond of you all, and why should I not confess it?

I need hardly tell you that I feel greatly honoured by this commission. Many thanks for your efforts.

Well now, let me just give you a brief outline of what is most necessary.

I have nothing pleasant to tell you about myself. I can well believe that my strange behaviour has startled you – I am not apologizing for it. No doubt the very bad weather is partly responsible for my condition. Formerly I used to be able to make all my other circumstances subservient to my art. I admit, however, that by so doing I became a bit crazy.

Gradually there comes to us the power to express just what we desire and feel – but how difficult is that for me! Perhaps the only touch of genius which

I possess is that my things are not always in very good order....

Forgive the trouble I am giving you. The tempo has been marked in pencil. Please do not forget it.

One thing more. Continue to raise yourself higher and higher into the divine realm of art. For there is no more undisturbed, more unalloyed or purer pleasure than that which comes from such an experience. Unfortunately we are dragged down from the supernatural element in art only too rudely into the earthly and human sides of life. It is a pity that this must be so, but that is all we can do. In this matter I shall remain true to my principles until I die.

And the conclusion? It should be as loud as possible. That is absolutely necessary. There must be no hesitation whatever about this. I know for certain that you will remember this.

Nothing else is required.

Make use of all these facts – I wish you every success.

JOB: AN ORATORIO

PART ONE

Prelude

No. 1. Chorus	God is here
	Near
	And divine
	Mind
	Speaks

No. 2. The Voice of GOD	Job – my Servant, my Son –
	I see into your Soul –
(Trio)	And can you visit mine?
	To view your very Self
	In Mirror Shine?
(with Chorus)	To view your very Self, &c.

51 – Part One

Everybody is here.

Yes, we are all here!

It is another crowd scene. Voices. People. In Boylston Hall that afternoon of Sunday October 27, 1833.

Old Graupner has come! Good for him! He doesn't go out much these days...

What will the musicians be doing, the orchestra, the chorus (the composer is speaking to them right now), the soloists, the conductor? Are there any rooms backstage or downstairs where they can make ready? If downstairs, is there a staircase leading up to the stage that will allow them to make their entrance with some degree of dignity? Or will they all have to be on stage by now, because there is nowhere else, some of them – the chorus – listening to the composer, even though some of them

No. 2a. Satan (*Tenor*)	What if you Changed?
No. 2. (*cont'd*)	I hear you, Light!
No. 2a. (*cont'd*)	What if you Changed? The Mirror clouded o'er – Might this Good Man Become an Evil-doer?
No. 2. (*cont'd*)	Proceed – Do what you may – Go on: my Man will stay. But keep your fire from him: Let him be – And let me.
No. 3. Chorus	Seized – every ox, every ass! Burned – every sheep on the grass! Thieved – every camel! Crushed as the house fell – Your children all.

understand not a word, while others – the orchestra – are tuning their instruments, testing reeds, adjusting the line of their attire, all of them part, with the audience, of the general hubbub, waiting for the moment of change – when the conductor comes forward, perhaps, or when they rise as he does so – that will convey them all, all, from the informal into the formal?

Yes, we are all here! Nearly all the members of the Society are here, of course, whether to perform or to listen, excepting only those who are visiting family, or away on business, or confined to their homes, this cold fall day, sitting with their feet in steaming mustard water or taking Moore's Essence of Life. Allan Pollock, maker of scientific instruments, is here. Increase Withington is here, to sing bass in the chorus. Ephraim Langdon Frothingham is here, future joint author with his son of *Philosophy as Absolute Science*. Jubal Howe the watchmaker is here. Charles Griffiths, of Welch, Griffiths, and Reeves, sawmakers, is not here. But P. P. Pond the shoemaker is here. And Lorenzo S. Cragin is here.

Lowell Mason comes to the front of the stage, where there is a tall desk, such as a clerk might use to stand at, with the bound score on it, closed, and raises his arms, looking out at the audience, to enjoin silence.

But there are more of us here than this, for certain. For certain, all of the city's professional musicians

No. 4. Job   I came into this world with nothing
(Bass)   And with nothing I shall go.
                          The lesson is the Lord's:
                          Bless the Lord.

No. 5. The Voice   No: Bless this Man that withstood!
of GOD   I have tested his Soul
(Chorus)   And found it fine.

No. 5a. Satan   What if you Changed?
(Tenor)

No. 5. *(cont'd)*   I hear you, Light!

No. 5a. *(cont'd)*   What if you Changed?
                          Let me at him?

No. 5. *(cont'd)*   Proceed – do what you will –
                          Let him ail –
                          And let me.

will be here, whether playing or in the audience, and so Eberle and Niebuhr will be here, and Dalmas, the French flutist. Oui, présent.

Or perhaps Mason has arranged for a room below from which the performers can come on, maybe to some applause, Mason entering last, certainly to some applause, to take his place at that same desk, the noise now falling away.

By no means only musicians will have been attracted to such an occasion. There are students from Harvard here, including John Sullivan Dwight, who later as a music critic will be a decisive and influential endorser of the composer for the U. S. public, and, in another section of the audience, a freshman still known as David Henry Thoreau. And surely Margaret Fuller is here, will have to be here.

Or perhaps Mason gives a signal to his players to start tuning, and it is that sound, of A, piped and bowed and boomed and blasted, in various registers, with various degrees of approximation, that brings the audience to hush.

No doubt the connoisseurs who attended the Jefferson auction of the preceding spring are here: Chester Harding himself, and Mrs. Davis, and Mr. Parkman, and Washington Allston, who will write of the event to Coleridge.

Our conductor will commence the proceedings with a few words, coughing loudly to gain attention,

No. 6. *(Chorus)*	Boils break through his skin To ooze searing salt! Hot blisters, cracked scabs – All signs of his guilt.
No. 7. Job's Wife *(Contralto)*	Is this the Justice of your God?
Interlude:	**The Silence of Job**
No. 8–1. **Job's Lament – 1**	Let that Day cease to exist That saw me born. May Time now wrinkle and crease And seal it down. What may I do If not die?
No. 9. Eliphaz *(Soprano)*	You were strong for so many – Why not for yourself? You have troubles so many – You earned them yourself. You have prayed for so many – Now pray for yourself.

and then saying how proud and honored the Society is that the composer not only deigned to accept the Society's commission but has fulfilled the terms of that commission in the most noble manner, and not only in so doing created a masterpiece for the ages but has come here to Boston to be present at the first performance, and here he gestures to the auditorium, and people start to clap and crane, and Thankful, sitting beside the composer, as so many times here before, taps him on the forearm and signs that he should rise, which he does, and the applause strengthens, and there may be cheers, and then it falls more rapidly after the composer has sat down again, until it has stopped.

And some have come here from further away. Longfellow is here. That bank messenger boy from New York, his return passage delayed by the storms, is here. And a woman has traveled on the stagecoach from Amherst, a hundred miles to the east – here she is, having left the baby at home, but with her four-year-old son sprawled against her, and her second child, her daughter a year younger, sitting neatly on the next chair, apart and aloof and alert.

Or perhaps the transition is more immediate. Mason raises his baton, tips it, and the music starts.

Thankful knows very well by now how it goes, how it will go. This time, though, it is different. This time, the hall packed with attentive hearers, the music not only being played but being absorbed

No. 8–2.
Job's Lament – 2

Arrows from God in my flesh
Are iron claws.
I reach out my hand and death
Slowly withdraws.
What may I do
If not die?

No. 10. Bildad
(*M.-Soprano*)

How long must you complain?
You think you are alone?
Bear in mind:
The good, they always prosper.
Look around:
The bad he will not spare.
Which then are you?

No. 8–3.
Job's Lament – 3

The voices round me speak
Words already said.
From empty mouths they talk;
Their wisdom is dead.
What may I do
If not die?

by others, and absorbing them, this time it is alive.
It is living. It breathes and sings. It speaks. That
beginning – the composer did not know quite
what to call it, and someone suggested "Prelude,"
which he liked, because the word reminded him
of Sebastian Bach. That beginning, slow, with the
violins striding high, at once tentative and resolute,
over other parts far below – cellos and double
basses, horns and bassoons, and intermittently a
quiet rumble from the timpani – all creating a space
the solo viola enters like someone coming in to a
strange but open city. That beginning already has
the new, fresh pulse of life.

And this life goes on into the opening chorus,
continuing without a break, as that solitary
clarinet carries the music on toward the fugue, the
continuing thread of life is felt by the soloists, felt
and maintained. Miss Belcher has never sounded
so clear, radiant. Marcus Colburn is justifying his
reputation. And now, for the first time, Thankful
understands that the theme of the fugue emerged
from the viola's peregrinations, its continuous
variations, which in retrospect she interprets as
trial runs, and that Mr. Colburn's seductive-sinister
responses echo that same guiding melodic principle,
as if to show the voice of the Divine comes from the
instrument, voiceless but singing, and how Satan
represents the Divine in distortion, in a distortion

No. 11. Zephar	I hurry to answer but what can I say?
(Contralto)	Can I speak for God?
	Who could know God's measure or
	where God may be
	Or when God will end?
	Perhaps God has gone now and will
	not return –
	What use your lament?

| **No. 8–4.** | God's limbs wind around the stars – |

Job's Lament – 4	What else is space?
	Divinity separates
	Itself from us.
	What may I do
	If not die?

End of the First Part

that then distorts the Divine itself, when the Divine condescends to respond to it.

Disarrayed by the Devil, God seems at the end of their dialogue almost to slink away, as the chorus comes rushing in again with news of the misfortunes that have senselessly been inflicted on Job: the loss of his entire livestock, the deaths, all at once, of his ten children. The movement is hectic, violent, soon over, and in its echo Mr. Richardson stands. He does not bewail his fate. He blames no-one. He stands, in the keenest adversity, to bless his Maker, in a majestic aria of affirmation. Mr. Richardson is always good here. Mr. Richardson is always good everywhere – firm, convincing. Here he surpasses what he could manage in rehearsal.

He sits down, and the fugue of the Divine voice is resumed, but with a difference, as if the Divine has heard the human and thereby been strengthened. However, Satan at this juncture appears more powerful than humanity, and the Divine is discommoded as it was before. Again there sweeps in a chorus, quick and forceful, that comes to a decisive halt, but, startlingly, one note of the final chord is held over by a lone female voice, emerging from the chorus to take the role of Job's wife. This singer is indeed Job's wife, Mrs. Richardson, chosen not for that connection but for the fullness of her low contralto, which easily overrides the four trombones that accompany her with unsettling harmonies – giving Thankful, as they always do, a sense of being assailed by something at once confused and intensely precise – as she declaims her eight syllables of outrage.

Mr. Richardson rises again – this time, however, not to sing but to stand, as the orchestra plays an adagio. During this, miraculously, God descends – or, at least, the three singers up in the balcony come down the spiral staircase to the stage. By the end of the movement, they have arrived, but Mr. Richardson has not acknowledged them, instead keeping his eyes ahead. When the music has died away completely, he begins as he did before, but his aria suddenly turns a different way as he calls for obliteration.

At this point – Thankful observed as much to the composer at one of the rehearsals last week, and he smiled and nodded – the drama changes from one of earth and heaven to one of earth alone, of human beings, two at a time: Job and one or other of his comforters, or confronters. Miss Belcher sings beautifully again, but what impresses Thankful more is how Mrs. Long, as the first comforter, though her three solos are all castigation, contrives to make her voice warm and appealing, even sympathetic. It is a long scene, lasting over half an hour and forming almost half this first part, but it has a deep continuity, maintained chiefly by Mr. Richardson's solos of adamant grief and bewilderment. There is every reason to admire, too, how the music makes it so that Job is simultaneously answering the comforters, one after another, and pursuing his own course. It is as if the comforters are offering invitations to dance, in figures of penitence and regret that circle only on themselves, always more or less fast than the main tempo – invitations that Job acknowledges while keeping to his steady walk, toward the massive hymn that is – though across at the beginning of the second part – its destination, where he will be joined at last by the chorus to make this a plea on behalf of all humanity.

52 – Intermission

"Is it really true? Are you here?"

"How could I have kept myself away, my dear friend?"

"I really cannot believe it!"

"I am afraid you have to. Here I am."

"I wanted to visit you, but unfortunately I could not find you."

"That may have been as well."

"The beautiful neckcloth, your own handiwork, came as a very great surprise to me."

"I am glad. It suits you. As I thought it would."

"How are you?"

"Better for being here. And you?"

"You see that I am always the same. What is one to do? The unfavorable weather constantly throws me back."

"It was summer before, when you were working with such furious energy."

"I have not forgotten."

"No more have I."

"Things are, however, very different with me now. In this most dreary, cold stormy weather, it is almost impossible to have any clear conceptions."

"I am very sorry indeed to hear –"

"Tomorrow or the day after I shall see you."

"I am afraid, my very dear friend, that will not be possible."

"Why not seize the moment, seeing that it flies so quickly?"

"Are you pleased with how the performance is going? Stupid question. Please forgive –"

"Everything went off tolerably well."

"There was a moment –"

"Where it runs thus:" [*sings*].

"Where cloud assumes a shape and changes it."

"Where I first saw the light."

"Where sunlight gathered."

"Where indeed all was *open*."

"Where winter lingers."

"Where I fail, or ever have failed."

"Where the lemons blossom."

"*The Devil take the whole business!*"

"The Devil has spoken, my dear friend – or, rather, he has sung."

"There must be something."

"My dear, dear friend, there truly *was* something. They are bringing it to birth here."

"It is very difficult to find a good libretto for an opera."

"I have laid down my pen, my friend. I could do no more."

"Do not refuse my request."

"I do not refuse it. I do not accede to it."

"I trust that when we meet again you will find that my art has made some progress in the interim."

"We will not meet again, my dearest friend. I will remain here, in Boston. This is my reality. You will return whence you came."

"Write to me now and then."

"You know that will not be possible. And yet we will meet again whenever and wherever this supreme work of yours is performed."

53 – Part Two

Almost certainly, nobody in the hall has heard the composer's Ninth Symphony. The work will not have a performance in the United States until 1846, and though some might have played through Czerny's piano-duet arrangement, that would scarcely have prepared them for what they are hearing now. Nor will anyone here – apart from the composer himself, to be sure – be familiar with the *Missa solemnis*. The Society is, yes, a choral institution, but one founded, also, on a particular religious affiliation, in a city where Congregationalist and Unitarian churches command almost universal adherence, inclining the musical inhabitants to favor oratorio in the German-English tradition, to the exclusion of other forms. This *Job* honors that tradition, for the composer knows it well – nor is he unaware of the religious character the city has inherited from its founders

of two centuries ago. Writing for the Handel and
Haydn Society, the composer has had both these
masters in his mind, but, lest there be any doubt,
there is something here, too, that is distinctly of
America, not of Europe but of elsewhere.

At the same time, the work that is now midway
through its first performance belongs to another
tradition, unattached to any place or convention: the
tradition of the composer's works, not least those
that are still relatively recent and scored for similar
forces. No-one in our own time would be able to
hear this oratorio except against the background of
the Ninth Symphony and the *Missa solemnis*, and by
no means only because of the evidently deliberate
allusions to those works present in the score. But the
only person in Boylston Hall this Sunday afternoon
possessing an awareness of that background, those
allusions – and what an awareness! – hears nothing
at all.

This may, for him, have its advantages. The
orchestra assembled by Lowell Mason numbers no
more than twenty players, and since it is unlikely
that four trombonists, for instance, are to be found
in all Sussex county, Charles Zeuner is having
to substitute for several instruments, besides
dealing with what is already hugely demanding
organ writing, unique in its period. Almost all
these musicians, Zeuner excepted, are, one should
remember, amateurs, people with other trades or

professions. The same is true of the chorus – and, indeed, the soloists, among whom only Marcus Colburn may be counted a professional singer. The composer has come to Boston to meet these musicians, observe them, gain some understanding of the musical-religious culture in which they exist, and attend their performance, but it is not specifically for them, in terms of their musical prowess, that he has written. By this point in his life, he well knows his stature. Perhaps he always did. The oratorio will live. It will be performed in Vienna, in London, in St. Petersburg, again here in Boston, and in cities yet unfounded. It will be acclaimed. It will be studied. It will excite amazement, and heavy recognition of its truth. This is just the beginning.

The beginning of this second part is crucial: a sequence of three chords, each immediately repeated and then followed by a long silence. The composer, seated once more, like everyone else, after the intermission's opportunities to get up and mingle, to talk about the magnificence and strangeness of the first part, or not, will know that everyone – not here, but later – will be thinking of *The Magic Flute*, a work that has come to mean more and more to him lately, but that everyone, too, having that model in mind, will be astonished, shaken, suddenly lifted into a new awareness. Or so he hopes – that the entire second part will unfold in a new place, a new space, its listeners changed.

PART TWO

No. 12.
Job's Hymn
(Tenor, with
Trio & Chorus
having no
words)

Why can my Voice not find You
Where may my Prayer be received
What should I hear in Your Silence –
How has my Mind been deceived?

Which of the Words I utter
Fails as it makes its Approach –
When will You give me an Answer,
Whether forgive or reproach?

No. 13.
Chorus

Think of this:
Against the men –
As will again –
A child stands

It is the finale of the Ninth Symphony that provides the most obvious point of comparison for this music of a kind unheard, because this is similarly music of overwhelming solidity, guaranteed by consistency of theme and type. The finale of the oratorio, however, is almost twice as long, lasting three quarters of an hour, and different both in the nature of its consistency and in the means by which that consistency is brought about. Where the last movement of the Ninth Symphony is underpinned by the character of a march, by D major jubilation, and by its sturdy theme, patterned on the alternation of eight syllables with an answering seven in the poem it sets, this second part of the oratorio is altogether more complex, as one must expect of a major work coming from the composer's fourth period and based on a text of a very different sort. Where the first stanza of Elihu's solo has the freshness of a folk song, other parts, even of this number, are densely worked, being at once harmonically adventurous and layered with history.

To this Boston audience, the music is untoward, beyond familiar reference points, and yet at the same time wondrous, perhaps most of all in its successions of harmonies, how they float, swerve or dive while also proceeding forward inexorably, how they keep their sights on that one sure path while sometimes veering to the side or soaring high above, carrying their first listeners into new air. Sitting in

No. 14.	Green goes my call as I sing from
Elihu's Song	tomorrow –
(Boy Soprano)	You think a youth should do no more than
	play?
	Weak is your argument, poor is your reason –
	Patient I stayed whilst you all had your say.

Given my powers by God, let me tell you
What you all know: how, in bed as you lay,
Ecstasy took you, and fear (you are shaking);
It was the Lord at your door on his way.

What made the primrose, the light, and the
mountain?
What made the night time, the morning,
the day?
How could you think such a one should
remember
All that you ask for, give all that you pray?

Interlude: **The Whirlwind**

No. 15. The Voice of GOD

(Chorus)   Where were you...

(Trio, severally)   ...to spin the stars and make the moon to
climb?

silent amazement in Boylston Hall, these people may lack experience enough to place what they hear in some larger context of the composer's output, but they respond to what is happening – sense what is happening to them – with an immediacy that may be the keener for their innocence.

Soon that innocence will be lost, and perhaps the music partly lost with it, scattered by the cutting winds of analysis and explanation, as these slice through to lay bare how the barely predictable splendor of this music, if often at times a grave splendor, depends on the composer's intensified study of Renaissance music, which allows him at last to attain, far beyond any straightforward imitation of the music of that era, three or four centuries in the past, a vast expansion of the resources of ordinary, existing tonality, the harmonic system based on major and minor scales. Those scales remain central, but their centrality is challenged and compromised and changed by simultaneous appeals to the scales of long-gone times – Phrygian, Dorian, Lydian, and the rest – re-entering as both ancient memory and fresh intelligence. There were intimations of this, of course, as far back as the Op. 132 string quartet, but within a far more limited ambit than the composer commands here in the second part of the oratorio, having meanwhile made a penetrating study of the music, in particular, of Heinrich Isaac. Communicating with abbeys in

(Chorus)	Where were you...
&c.	...to place the cloud upon the sea's expanse?
	...to see what was as time began to move?
	...to comprehend the language of the hind?
	...to frame a doorway down or up to death?
	...to tie Orion's belt or to undo?
	...to reckon up the treasures of the snow?
	...to fix the Laws by which all things abide?
	...to set the workings of the human brain?

Interlude (cont'd)

| **No. 16. Job** | Lord, I am vile; |
| (*Bass*) | I place my hand over my mouth. |

No. 17.	Rise up again.
The Voice	Were I a whale, could you find me food?
of GOD	Build me an abode?
(*Trio with*	Understand my word?
Chorus)	Make yourself understood?

No. 18. Job	Wonders...
(*Bass*)	...to have seen...
	...Pride in my Spirit...
	...and Unworthiness in my Soul.

various parts of Austria, the composer has acquired copies of masses and motets by the foremost musician at work in the empire under Maximilian, in the years around 1500. This music, coupled with that of Schubert's last months, offered him a bridge into the new style that is exemplified most fully and richly in the oratorio's finale.

What also helped was the text. The ascription of this to Hosea Ballou, a Boston cleric, must be set aside, as there is nothing in Ballou's ample published verse, mainly comprising hymnlike poems of an excitable piety, to prepare one for the irregular phrases, including very short lines, and the slant rhymes that plainly have had such a powerful effect on the composer's rhythm and formal structure. Indeed, the rhythmic-formal aspects of this finale are as remarkable and unprecedented as the melodic-harmonic – which, also, they serve to instigate and to justify. One may say that the composer here, as before only with Goethe and Schiller, finds a poet who is his equal. To consider Ballou in this context is absurd.

Just as the finale of the Ninth Symphony would have been inconceivable without the lines of Schiller to help guide and motivate it, that of the oratorio everywhere shows its great debt – and its great gratitude – to the anonymous libretto. To take up the comparison with the Ninth Symphony, where the finale of that work is most essentially a march,

No. 19. **The Voice** **of GOD** *(Trio with* *Chorus)*	Come forward the three false friends! You were ignorance abusing knowledge; You were folly rebuking wisdom; You were closed against the true.
No. 19a. **Satan** *(Tenor)*	*[aside]* I am struck dumb.
No. 19. *(cont'd)*	Make a fire To burn up what you have most desired!

Interlude: The Sacrifice

No. 20. **Chorus**	And Job had his reward, To be restored To all he had had And still more. The comforters left And the whirlwind went. Job stood. Job stood. Job stood.

End of the Oratorio

this second part of the oratorio is in the nature of a sarabande, if one that flashes with speed and variety on occasion. And where the earlier movement is based on a theme that keeps coming back more or less in its original form, the "theme," if such it can be called, of the oratorio finale is a continuously mutable essence, one whose presence may be heard even in the melody of Elihu's aria:

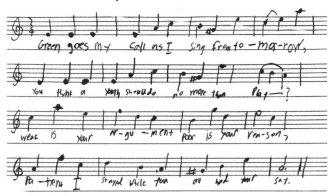

Here the composer, with characteristic creative economy, recalls a line he sketched back in May 1820. If this is the earliest, and therefore in a sense the original form of the finale theme, it comes from a time when he cannot have imagined the wealth he would be able to draw from this material thirteen years later.

Even the above short excerpt may indicate the encouragement the composer received from his poet – and, conceivably, vice versa, for there is a persuasive view that the libretto was written by someone in constant contact with the composer at the time, responding to his wishes. Though shaped of necessity by the Biblical source, the text seems to be paying close attention to the composer's requirements, as well as to those of his principal singer. After steering through the colossal lament of the first part, the solo bass (or tenor, should the composer's rumored alternative version come to light) is asked to sing only the hymn that opens the second part – massive as this number is – and a couple of short solos toward the end. His last contribution comes as a delayed answer to, or resolution of, the much more florid and extensive solo for Elihu, a solo that, for its demands on strength, range, rhythmic precision, and variety of expressive color, is unrivaled in the repertory for boy soprano. No account of the première, whether in printed report, diary, or private correspondence, fails to mention the impression made by the role's first exponent, Lowell Mason, Jr.

The voice heard most through this closing half of the oratorio, however, is that of God, brought back from the silence into which he withdrew in the first part. Satan is reduced to a single line, though a crucial one, whose final syllable is extended into a long and increasingly agitated humming vocalise that continues all the way into the final orchestral interlude. Where God's voice is concerned, the

balance has shifted in favor of the solid magnificence of the eight-part chorus, only occasionally
now joined by, or giving way to, the trio of high
soprano, soprano, and mezzo-soprano directed to
sing from aloft, and heard thus soon after the start
of the opening half.

It is about God, Thankful thinks, as she listens. It
is about this universe in which God is omnipotent.
And it is about a larger universe in which God is
powerless, helpless.

54 – Departure

They will be back on Lewis Wharf, the three gentlemen from the Society – Richardson, Chickering, and Mason – and the composer, just as before, and surely there will be a coachman with them to take care of the composer's baggage, and Thankful will be there, to transmit the gentlemen's final salutes of thanks and praise and well-wishing. It will be a more or less conventional scene, given a little tweak by how Thankful will not be a totally transparent medium, but will sign, as she has increasingly, just the essence of what someone will say, together with her own commentary, which will cause the composer to incline his head and smile, gestures that the interlocutor will take as expressive of approval or interest or amusement or whatever the interlocutor wishes. They will all laugh. They will all watch as the coachman passes the composer's chest to the oarsman standing in the wherry, and as both help the composer aboard. They will wave as the composer is rowed out to the brig in the bay that will take him back to Europe.

Thankful, who will have, like anyone else, an interior voice she hears in silence, will also sometimes have her mind relaying messages to her by way of signs. So it will be. Keeping her gaze on the ship as it rounds the headland and disappears, she will also see, in her inner void, these speaking hands: "Did it all really happen?"

Notes

Words attributed to Beethoven, throughout, are taken as complete clauses – and, in most cases, complete sentences – from his letters, as translated in one or other of the following sources:

Lady Wallace, trans.: *Beethoven's Letters* (1790-1826) (London: Longmans, Green, 1866) [W]

A. C. Kalischer, ed.; J. S. Shedlock, trans.: *The Letters of Ludwig van Beethoven* (London: Dent, 1909) [K]

Emily Anderson, trans.: *The Letters of Beethoven* (London: Macmillan, 1961) [A]

Thanks to Guido Gorna for checking the German, Rupert Griffiths for remembering there was a sign language on Martha's Vineyard, Stephanie Vyce for supplying a copy of Nora Ellen Groce's book, and Bobby Barañano for the manuscript reproduced on p.285.

4

August 9, 1812, Breitkopf & Härtel [A 380].

6

October 6, 1802, Carl and Johann van Beethoven
[W 26].

12

December 1817, Nanette Streicher [A 844].

13

July 22-6, 1822, Johann van Beethoven [A 1086]; June 29,
1801, Franz Gerhard Wegeler [A 51]; n.d., Anton Schindler [W
332]; July 6, 1804, Gottlob Wiedebein [A 90]; October 9, 1811,
Breitkopf & Härtel [A 325]; n.d., Karl van Beethoven [W 447];
June 28, 1812, Joseph Anton Ignaz von Baumeister [A 371];
December 1815, Sigmund Anton Steiner [A 578]; March 10,
1823, Nikolaus Simrock [A 1153]; 1814, Baroness Dorothea
von Ertmann [A 516]; September 20, 1807, Countess Josephine
Deym [A 151]; 1798, Nikolaus Zmeskall von Domanovecz
[A 30]; May 15, 1816, Countess Anna Marie Erdődy [A 634];
August 1819, Joseph Karl Bernard [A 969]; September 5, 1823,
Ferdinand Ries [A 1237]; early November, 1815, Antonia
Brentano [A 570]; May 3, 1825, Heinrich Rellstab [A 1366b];
September 1815, Sigmund Anton Steiner [A 561].

15

Descriptions of lots are transcribed from the catalog, with
grateful thanks to the library of the Boston Athenaeum for

supplying this in digitized form. The John Adams portrait is in the collection of the same institution, whose website provides information used here.

19

February 8, 1823, Zelter [W 315]; before February 18, 1820, Johann Baptist Bach [A 1006]; October 13, 1826, Tobias Haslinger [W 461]; c. May, 1820, Tobias Haslinger [A 1025]; May 27, 1813, Archduke Rudolph [W 110]; n.d., Baroness Thérèse von Drossdick [W 61]; May 8, 1812, Joseph von Varena [A 369]; September 18, 1810, Johann Andreas Streicher [A 275]; August 22, 1814, Johann Nepomuk Kanka [A 486].

20

July 6, 1800, Countess Giulietta Guicciardi [W 15].

23

The Wampanoag *wushówunan* = hawk; see Roger Williams: *A Key into the Language of America: or, An Help to the Language of the Natives in that Part of America, called New-England* (London, 1643), p. 95.

25

Mid-November, 1819, Joseph Karl Bernard [A 983]; end of February, 1827, Anton Schindler [W 467]; October 19, 1815, Countess Anna Marie Erdődy [A 563]; January 28, 1812, Breitkopf & Härtel [A 345]; autumn 1817, Nanette Streicher [W 245]; November 16, 1801, Franz Gerhard Wegeler [A 54]; July 6, 1822, Ferdinand Ries [A 1084]; October 7, 1826, Franz Gerhard Wegeler [W 459]; July 16, 1823, Ferdinand Ries [A

1209]; July 24, 1813, Archduke Rudolph [W 111]; May 6, 1810, Johann Andreas Streicher [A 257]; May 25, 1813, Ignaz Franz Castelli [A 423].

28

March 1803, Ferdinand Ries [A 71]; June 9, 1801, Franz Gerhard Wegeler [A 51]; February 10, 1811, Bettina Brentano [W 67]; July 1, 1801, Karl Amenda [A 53]; 1818, Nikolaus Zmeskall von Domanovecz [A 928]; March 7, 1821, Adolf Martin Schlesinger [A 1050]; February 13, 1814, Count Franz Brunsvik [A 462]; August 15, 1812, Bettina von Arnim [W 93]; March 10, 1815, Breitkopf & Härtel [A 533]; December 1817, Tobias Haslinger [A 843]; August 21, 1805, Nikolaus Zmeskall von Domanovecz [A 805]; September 20, 1807, Countess Josephine Deym [A 151]; July 16, 1823, Ferdinand Ries [A 1209]; August 26, 1804, Breitkopf & Härtel [A 96]; October 18, 1802, Breitkopf & Härtel [A 62]; December 1816, Tobias Haslinger [A 695]; spring 1810, Baron Ignaz von Gleichenstein [A 254]; December 1804, Countess Josephine Deym [A 103]; autumn 1807, Countess Josephine Deym [A 156]; May 6, 1810, Johann Andreas Streicher [A 257]; June 6, 1810, Breitkopf & Härtel [A 261]; May 23, 18??, Karl van Beethoven [W 420]; October 6, 1824, Tobias Haslinger [A 1315]; June 5, 1822, Carl Friedrich Peters [A 1079].

There was a *Job* oratorio of approximately this period, written by William Russell in 1814 and performed at the Foundling Hospital in London, where the composer was organist. See Katharine J. Dell: "Nineteenth-Century British Job Oratorios," *Interested Readers: Essays on the Hebrew Bible in Honor of David J.*

A. Clines, ed. James K. Aitken, Jeremy M. S. Clines, and Christl
M. Maier (Atlanta: Society of Biblical Literature, 2013), pp.
415-29.

31

August 29, 1824, Karl van Beethoven [W 386]; summer 1823,
Anton Schindler [A 1223]; September 5, 1823, Ferdinand Ries
[A 1237]; January 23, 1824, Gesellschaft der Musikfreunde,
Vienna [A 1260]; February 13, 1814, Count Franz Brunsvik [A
462]; October 9, 1813, Nikolaus Zmeskall von Domanovecz
[A 434]; spring 1805, Countess Josephine Deym [A 110];
1823, Archduke Rudolph [W 353]; February 25, 1824, Moritz
Schlesinger [A 1267]; April, 1825, Hofrat Karl Peters [A 1360].
Details of Hannah Hill's parentage and upbringing come from
the page on the Quincy-Hill-Phillips-Treadwell Papers on the
website of the Cambridge Historical Society.

33

c. September 18, 1803, Hoffmeister & Kühnel [A 82]; March
1803, Ferdinand Ries [A 71]; April 1809, Baron Ignaz von
Gleichenstein [A 213]; March 28, 1809, Johann van Beethoven
[A 205]; November 1819, Vincenz Hauschka [A 981]; July
1814, Carl von Adlersburg [A 485]; January 14, 1815, Johann
Nepomuk Kanka [A 522]; soon after June 23, 1807, Baron
Ignaz von Gleichenstein [A 148]; July 1817, Nanette Streicher
[A 794]; early January, 1818, Nanette Streicher [A 885];
Autumn 1804, Stephan von Breuning [A 98]; April 25, 1823,
Ferdinand Ries [A 1167]; March 1809, Countess Anna Marie
Erdődy [A 207]; 1817, Nanette Streicher [A 849]; January 2,

1810, Breitkopf & Härtel [A 243]; February 19, 1811, Breitkopf
& Härtel [A297]; May 17, 1825, Karl van Beethoven [A 1372].

34

For basic facts on Aaron Hill (though the name of his wife is
given incorrectly) see the page headed "The Thirtieth Meeting
– Volume Nine" on the website of the Cambridge Historical
Society. Further information about Hannah Hill's family is
taken from: *History of Cambridge, Massachusetts, 1630-1877, with
a Genealogical Register by Lucius R. Paige. Supplement and Index
by Mrs. Mary Isabella Gozzaldi* (Cambridge, Mass.: Cambridge
Historical Society, 1930), pp. 380-86.

35

1809, Freiherr von Hammer-Purgstall [W 59].
Josiah Quincy did indeed invite Longfellow to Harvard in
December 1834.

36

July 24, 1813, Archduke Rudolph [A 429].

37

June 13, 1807, Baron Ignaz von Gleichenstein [A 144];
February 17, 1827, Franz Gerhard Wegeler [W 464]; April
8, 1815, Johann Nepomuk Kanka [W 148]; July 1, 1801, Karl
Amenda [A 53]; February 5, 1823, Ferdinand Ries [A 1133];
January 1811, Therese Brunsvik [A 295]; November 19, 1796,
Johann Andreas Streicher [A 17]; February 1808, ? Heinrich
Joseph von Collin [A 164]; June 1794, Johann Schenk [A

11]; June 23, 1807, Baron Ignaz von Gleichenstein [A 146]; January 2, 1810, Breitkopf & Härtel [A 243]; October 1, 1797, Lorenz von Breuning [A 21]; 1794-6, Franz Gerhard Wegeler [A 15]; March 5, 1807, Paul and Marie Bigot de Morogues [A 140]; August 15, 1812, Bettina von Arnim [W 93]; May 1810, Therese Malfatti [A 258]; March 8, 1819, Ferdinand Ries [A 938]; September 22, 1816, Cajetan Giannatasio del Rio [A 658]; October 1816, Karl van Beethoven [A 667]; Summer 1808, Baron Ignaz von Gleichenstein [A 173]; late November, 1816, Karl van Beethoven [A 673]; April 23, 1813, Nikolaus Zmeskall von Domanovecz [A 417]; 1816, Nikolaus Zmeskall von Domanovecz [A 715]; August 14, 1817, Cajetan Giannatasio del Rio [A 800]; end of March, 1817, Johann Nepomuk Kanka [A 771]; n.d., Karl van Beethoven [W 432]; 1824, Tobias Haslinger [A 1340]; August 31, 1822, Johann van Beethoven [A 1094]; May 17, 1825, Karl van Beethoven [A 1372]; June 9, 1825, Karl van Beethoven [A 1386].

38
1818, Count Moritz von Dietrichstein [A 929].

39
1816, Countess Anna Marie Erdődy [A 722]; April 25, 1809, Nikolaus Zmeskall von Domanovecz [A 215]; July 1, 1801, Karl Amenda [A 53]; March 5, 1807, Paul Bigot de Morogues [A 138a]; August 21, 1805, Nikolaus Zmeskall von Domanovecz [A 805]; August 1817, Nanette Streicher [A 810]; shortly before November 6, 1825, ? Karl Holz [A 1450]; April 8, 1815, Johann Nepomuk Kanka [A 540]; May 1810, Therese Malfatti [A 258];

February 1817, Cajetan Giannatasio del Rio [A 767]; July 13, 1825, Karl van Beethoven [A 1397]; February 6, 1816, Antonia Brentano [A 607]; September 27, 1826, Tobias Haslinger [A 1528]; c. 1807, Paul Bigot de Morogues [A 161]; May 27, 1813, Archduke Rudolph [A 426]; c. March 1803, Ferdinand Ries [A 69]; June 1803, Ferdinand Ries [A 78]; 1816, Joseph von Varena [A 721]; shortly after July 20, 1815, Countess Anna Marie Erdődy [A 549].

40

April 9, 1825, Ferdinand Ries [W 403]; August 1825, Karl Holz [A 1421]; December 26, 1823, Ignaz Moscheles [A 1245]; [A 1421]; April 1809, Baron Ignaz von Gleichenstein [A 216].

41

August 1825, Karl Holz [A 1421]; January 27, 1827, Bernhard Schotts Söhne [A 1548]; [A 1421]; June 3, 1823, Moritz Schlesinger [A 1190]; May 6, 1811, Breitkopf & Härtel [A 306]; n.d., n.p. [W 71]; August 21, 1817, Nikolaus Zmeskall von Domanovecz [A 805].

42

August 3, 1820, Archduke Rudolph [K 810].

44

June 14, 1825, Karl van Beethoven [A 1389].

45

Late July, 1823, Archduke Rudolph [A 1214]; March 14, 1827, Ignaz Moscheles [W 473]; December 20, 1820, Carlo Boldrini [A 1040]; April 8, 1813, Joseph von Varena [A 414].

Everything by Ballou comes from his sermon "Unity of God, or Controversy Decided," published in his *Nine Sermons on Important Doctrinal and Practical Subjects Delivered in Philadelphia, November, 1834* (Philadelphia: Abel C. Thomas, 1835), pp. 35-46. One of Thankful's speeches is from the same source.

47

A visit to a rehearsal in 1837 by "a number of Indian chiefs" is recorded in *History of the Handel and Haydn Society, of Boston, Massachusetts* (Boston: Alfred Mudge & Son, 1883-93). The visitors "were especially delighted with the organ, which they conceived to be the abode of the Great Spirit."

Three words are taken from Josiah Cotton: *Vocabulary of the Massachusett (or Natick) Indian Language* (Cambridge: E. W. Metcalf, 1829): *wonkŭssis* = fox, *pohkintippŏhkod* = dark night, *penoowinneunkqusspinneat* = to be changed.

48

1815, Sigmund Anton Steiner [A 589]; April 3, 1826, Gottfried Weber [W 451]; n.d., Georg Friedrich Treitschke [W 121]; November 2, 1793, Eleonore von Breuning [W 4]; July 14, 1802, Hoffmeister & Kühnel [A 60]; 1796, Johann Andreas Streicher [A 18]; 1809, Nikolaus Zmeskall von Domanovecz [A 235]; April 1814, Nikolaus Zmeskall von Domanovecz [A 476]; c. March 1804, Joseph Sonnleithner [A 88]; Summer 1808,

Baron Ignaz von Gleichenstein [A 173]; end of August 1823, Anton Schindler [A 1236]; July 15, 1817, Wilhelm Gerhard [A 788]; May 27, 1813, Joseph von Varena [A 424]; c. October 22, 1816, Sigmund Anton Steiner [A 665]; 1816, Cajetan Giannatasio del Rio [W 172]; September 17, 1812, Breitkopf & Härtel [A 383]; December 1809, Breitkopf & Härtel [A 232]; December 28, 1816, Johann Nepomuk Kanka [A 686]; July 15, 1819, Archduke Rudolph [A 952]; February 28, 1816, Ferdinand Ries [W 169]; July 17, 1812, Breitkopf & Härtel [A 375]; July 5, 1806, Breitkopf & Härtel [A 132]; June 12, 1825, Tobias Haslinger [W 380]; 1816, Nikolaus Zmeskall von Domanovecz [A 715]; n.d., Karl van Beethoven [W 433]; July 13, 1825, Johann van Beethoven [A 1398].

"It was not the same in the song": Melville quotes from his own *Moby-Dick*.

49

Probably 1817, to Giannatasio del Rio [K 671].

50

Summer 1826, Karl Holz [A 1516]; March 5, 1807, Paul Bigot de Morogues [A 138a]; February 19, 1816, Nikolaus Zmeskall von Domanovecz [A 608]; February 1810, Baron Ignaz von Gleichenstein [A 247]; March 7, 1821, Adolf Martin Schlesinger [A 1050]; 1809, Nikolaus Zmeskall von Domanovecz [A 238]; [A 138a]; 1817, Archduke Rudolph [A 854]; c. February, 1818, Nanette Streicher [A 894]; July 1, 1823, Archduke Rudolph [A 1203]; May 13, 1816, Countess Anna Marie Erdődy [A 633]; April 22, 1801, Franz Anton

Hoffmeister [A 47]; March 1813, Nikolaus Zmeskall von Domanovecz [A 408]; July 16, 1816, Sigmund Anton Steiner [A 641]; August 14, 1817, Cajetan Giannatasio del Rio [A 800]; August 19, 1817, Xaver Schnyder von Wortensee [A 803]; late July 1825, Prince Nikolay Galitsin [A 1405]; November 1816, Sigmund Anton Steiner [A 677]; June 10, 1825, Joseph Karl Bernard [A 1387]; early August, 1819, Joseph Karl Bernard [A 958]; July 7, 1817, Nanette Streicher [A 785]; April 8, 1803, Breitkopf & Härtel [A 72]; c. July 20, 1804, Ferdinand Ries [A 93]; 1816, Johanna van Beethoven [A 727]; November 13, 1802, Breitkopf & Härtel [A 63]; March 5, 1818, Ferdinand Ries [A 895].

52

April 1809, Baron Ignaz von Gleichenstein [A 213]; c. May 1820, Tobias Haslinger [A 1025]; 1809, Nikolaus Zmeskall von Domanovecz [A 241]; c. early June 1794, Eleonore von Breuning [A 9]; January 23, 1810, Nikolaus Zmeskall von Domanovecz [A 244]; spring 1823, Johann van Beethoven [A 1164]; late July 1823, Archduke Rudolph [A 1214]; August 23, 1824, Archduke Rudolph [W 385]; November 1819, Vincenz Hauschka [A 981]; February 22, 1827, Ignaz Moscheles [W 466]; May 17, 1825, Karl van Beethoven [A 1372]; September 20, 1807, Countess Josephine Deym [A 151]; c. March 4, 1807, Marie Bigot de Morogues [A 138]; 1810, Baron Ignaz von Gleichenstein [A 287]; n.d., n.p. [W 407]; June 29, 1800, Franz Gerhard Wegeler [W 14]; 1812, Freiherr Joseph von Schweiger [W 89]; May 27, 1813, Archduke Rudolph [W 110]; January 1, 1814, Nikolaus Zmeskall von Domanovecz [A 456]; [A 456];

June 11, 1811, Count Ferdinand Pálffy [A 312]; January 28, 1812, August von Kotzebue [A 344]; July 9, 1810, Nikolaus Zmeskall von Domanovecz [W 65]; August 2, 1794, Nikolaus Simrock [A 12].

The phrases beginning "Where" are not, of course, complete sentences on Beethoven's part, while the other speaker here quotes from poems by Goethe.

53

Beethoven notated the melody in one of his conversation books, in the first half of May 1820. In Giovanni Biamonti's exhaustive catalog, *Catalogo cronologico e tematico delle opere di Beethoven, comprese quelle inedite e gli abbozzi non utilizzati* (Turin: ILTE, 1968), it has the number 726. Attempts were made by the publisher to find the copyright holder, but the company appears to have become bankrupt.

54

Following the performance, the musical materials would have been returned to the office of Charles Bradlee and so lost in the fire there five days later (information from Wikisource).

PAUL GRIFFITHS is a music critic, librettist, and novelist. The author of many books about Western classical music, he has been a music critic for *The Times* (London), *The New Yorker*, and *The New York Times*, among other places. He is a member of the American Academy of Arts and Sciences and has been honored by the British and French governments for his services to literature and composition. Griffiths's other novels are *Myself and Marco Polo*, *The Lay of Sir Tristam*, and *let me tell you*, which was excerpted in *The Penguin Book of Oulipo*. On December 16, 2019, Griffiths opened the worldwide 2020 celebration of the 250th anniversary of Beethoven's birth with a text commissioned for performance by the Beethovenorchester, Bonn: "O Freunde, nicht diese Töne!"